THE CHRONICLES OF KITCHIKE

THE CHRONICLES OF KITCHIKE

TAKING A HARD FALL

LOUIS-KARL PICARD-SIOUI

TRANSLATED BY
KATHRYN GABINET-KROO

singular fiction, poetry, nonfiction, translation, drama, and graphic books

Library and Archives Canada Cataloguing in Publication

Title: The chronicles of Kitchike : taking a hard fall / Louis-Karl Picard-Sioui ; translated by Kathryn Gabinet-Kroo.
Other titles: Chroniques de Kitchike. English
Names: Picard-Sioui, Louis-Karl, 1976- author.
Description: Short stories. | Translation of: Chroniques de Kitchike.
Identifiers: Canadiana (print) 20220405581 | Canadiana (ebook) 20220405611 | ISBN 9781550969931 (softcover) | ISBN 9781550969962 (EPUB) | ISBN 9781550969986 (Kindle) | ISBN 9781550969993 (PDF)
Classification: LCC PS8631.I33 C4713 2022 | DDC C843/.6—dc23

Cover and pages designed by Michael Callaghan
Cover art by Hare Krishna/Shutterstock
Typeset in Fairfield and Trajan Pro fonts at Moons of Jupiter Studios
Published by Exile Editions Ltd ~ www.ExileEditions.com
144483 Southgate Road 14 – GD, Holstein, Ontario, N0G 2A0
Printed and bound in Canada by Imprimerie Gauvin

Conseil des Arts du Canada Canada Council for the Arts

ONTARIO CREATES

We gratefully acknowledge the financial support of the Canada Council for the Arts, the Government of Canada, and Ontario Creates toward our publishing activities.

Canadian sales representation:
The Canadian Manda Group,
664 Annette Street, Toronto ON M6S 2C8.
www.mandagroup.com 416 516 0911

North American and international distribution, and U.S. sales:
Independent Publishers Group,
814 North Franklin Street,
Chicago IL 60610 www.ipgbook.com
toll free: 1 800 888 4741

FSC www.fsc.org MIX Paper FSC® C100212

All peoples cover with snow
the stained arrows in their history

When our hearts grow cold
the shared silence
will conceal our lies

Jean Sioui, *L'Avenir voit rouge*

KITCHIKE NURSERY RHYME

a dreamcatcher hangs from the mirror of yer auto
works at night when you sleep in it, all blotto
dead drunk and countin' stars til dawn,
yessirree, your money's all gone
and the Gas Bar has banned you
no sweat, Uncl' Jake is the chef
he keeps an eye out for you, he knows what's best
says "get your feathers, your fringes, an' dress yourself up
burn some sage for the Minister, then heave a sigh and a puff
dance a step to the left, and one to the right
put on a good show so the money will flow
then believe me, you'll be up real up late, Joe!"

PROLOGUE

Dong! Ding dong!

Whoa that hurts! Saint-Gabriel-of-Kitchike wakes me up with the clamorous tolling of its bell. My head wants to split in two. My body is encased in the depths of the mattress, the sheets are drenched, and my mouth is dry. I'm pretty sure I swallowed an ashtray. I grit my teeth so I can crack an eye open. There's a fan spinning on the ceiling. Fuck, I'm not at home. That's for damn sure. I close my squinty eye before the rotating blades make me sick to my stomach. Pierre Wabush, you big dope, you shouldn't drink so much. Then you wouldn't have to spend these days-after-the night-before contemplating the void.

Dong! Ding dong! Dong!

Christ Almighty, no way I can go back to sleep with that bell up to its usual tricks.

I stretch my arm out and gingerly pat the sheets, a little further, always further, until my fingers reach the edge of the mattress. Good, at least you're the only wreck washed up in this bed. No one else will have to smell your bad breath. Still, I wouldn't mind knowing where it is that I ran aground this time around.

Let's rewind last night to figure it out.

A little spring bonfire at Jakob's to celebrate the homecoming of Teandishru'. Our national darling is beginning to take himself a little too seriously, but whatever. A friend is a friend, plus he's a damn good guitarist. He attracts the curious and the groupies, not just the regular gang hanging around at the end of the night. So there's that, plus the dozen or so pallets that we arranged in the blaze.

So, who was there? The guys from the shop, for sure. Old Noé, who entertained us with his silly antics and his stories. Max Yaskawish, the owner of the Gas Bar, because naturally the Tooktoo clan had to be represented. Young Brokenheart is the pride of the whole community. He's probably one of the very few who could make something like that happen. Even Roméo, the local shaman, passed by to celebrate the end of his nephew's tour. He rarely attends such events on this back-of-beyond reserve.

Dong! Ding dong! Dong!

Focus, Wabush! You're not in Old Méo's bed, that's for sure.

Which of the ladies had been there? Jean-Paul's girlfriend, that much I remember. She spent the whole time watching him to make sure he didn't drink. Unlikely that she took me home with her. Little Beth from Basse-Côte, come to play groupie. She'd never stoop so low as to hook up with me. Aside from those two, there were the girls from the mini-mart: Stephanie, Charles's ex I wouldn't touch that – Sophie Tooktoo and Lydia.

Lydia. Lydia Yaskawish, obviously.

"LYDIA?"

Dong! Ding dong! Dong!

No answer.

I yell a little louder to compete with the bell. But I'm fairly sure there's no one in the place.

I use the back of my hand to clear the grit from my sleepy eyes and somehow find the strength to sit up. The walls are a scarlet red, the furniture made of plywood, and Justin Timberlake posters are pinned up near those of Sitting Bull. No doubt about it, I'm at Lydia's. Again. I have to remember to stop doing this. It's easier to recall such details when you wake up with a hangover than when you're drunk. And have a hard-on. In any case, it's beginning to seem too much like a habit.

I peel my ass off the bed and start looking for my shorts and the rest of my gear. I never was any good at treasure hunts, especially when my head's about to explode. I finally decided to start this game of hide-and-seek in the bathroom.

Wait, she left me a Post-it on the medicine cabinet: *Don't touch the blue ones.*

Hey, she's getting to know me a little too well! But since I respect her, I settle for the whites and the reds.

They aren't Smarties, so I don't have to save them for last.

The bell has fallen silent so I shouldn't need them anymore, but I take no chances.

I do three tours of the apartment to locate my clothes. I find my shorts in the sheets, my T-shirt in the hall, and my underwear in the living room.

Must have been more rock 'n' roll than you thought, eh, Wabush?

I raise a leg to pull on my underwear but when I put my foot down, I feel the cold slip-sliding of a little metal chassis and I swear my ass off. Jesus Christ! The pain in my head drops all the way to my tailbone.

Fuck Lydia, I'm taking the blues anyway. You'll just have to tell your little scar-face not to leave his Hot Wheels on the carpet.

I stand up, holding my breath and convincing myself that it doesn't hurt that badly, then see another Post-it on the living room table: *Watch out for the trucks.*

I couldn't help laughing.

Time to sever the ties.

Just then, my telephone begins to vibrate.

Oh, no! Wabush, do not answer it. You know the rule. The next day, you leave without a trace, no one any the wiser. She may be young and sexy, and she knows how to make me laugh even when she's not there, but I'm not ready to park my pickup in the same garage every night. Especially if it means playing substitute dad with little Waso. If I'd wanted a family, I'd have had one before I turned 40. I never wanted to make my offspring suffer the torments of Kitchike. That's no heritage to pass on: Lost between the city and the reserve, our glorious past and our colonized present, with no dreams and no hope, caught up in our bickering over bells, surrounded by pondfuls of racist Frogs, under little Canadian princes' code of silence. Starting life with two strikes against you? I wouldn't wish that on anyone.

I pick my sweater up off the TV. I put on the one sock found lying in the hallway, but even after searching the entire apartment, I can't find its mate. I'm pretty sure I was wearing two socks when I went out yesterday.

Fuck, I'm not going to spend the whole day here either. Especially since I'm starting to get hungry.

Just as I go the fridge and grab the handle, my cell phone buzzes, making me jump. Oh, God, look at this! She left me a message. Just what I need. My stomach sends me its own noisy notification, so I decide to open the fridge door. I can't help but smile. On the top shelf, just under a package of smoked moose slices, there it is: my missing sock. And of course, one last yellow Post-it.

Surprise!

Damn that Lydia. It really is time for me to scram. I put on my other sock, which is really much too cold for comfort, and scarf down the sliced moose meat. I assume it was meant as a gift, but in the worst-case scenario, I'll consider it my sweet revenge.

I'll admit that at this point, I have a moment of weakness. Or clarity. Or just plain curiosity. Whatever. Suddenly I want to know, so I unlock my cell and listen to the message. It's not from Lydia, unless her voice has changed overnight. Nope, it's a man, and I'm fairly sure that I don't know him: "Geronimo, the old guy told me you're game. I'll wait for you at the Halloway. On the 17th, at midnight. Watch for a mauve-coloured scarf. And be subtle about it."

A shiver runs through my body. I'm convinced it's nothing to do with my refrigerated sock. So, they weren't just rumours...

That's when it happens. The change of regime. Divine justice is going to rain down on our community and it looks like you'll be the one who has to carry the sword. You're going to have to put your money where your mouth is, Pierre, old boy. It's now or never.

I put my cell back in my pocket and go to leave, but just before I open the door, I can't help but stop in front of the staged photo on the wall in the foyer. A radiant Lydia with little Waso in her arms. He couldn't have been more than two at the time. He didn't have the scar yet. He was beautiful and perfect.

Kitchike has a way of perverting anything beautiful and good. For ripping your body open so that you muck about in your own guts. Wabush, the only legacy you ever wanted to leave was the truth that we exist. That we are still here. There are little kids like Waso who have to grow up here, have to survive here.

I don't know if it's because of the Post-its, the moose meat she left for me, the Hot Wheels ride or just because it was the day after a bender, but I suddenly feel tears welling up. Tears of impudent rage. I was thinking that if there was something I could do with my shitty life to give our kids a chance to flourish on our no-man's-land of a reserve, I wouldn't hesitate to do it.

The countdown has started.

I slam the door shut.

Watch out, Kitchike.

JEAN-PAUL PAUL JEAN-PIERRE

Jean-Paul Paul Jean-Pierre had risen one fine day and noticed that a gaping hole had moved in with him. No time to make a coffee or toast a slice of bread or even smoke a cigarette. The black hole had invited itself in early that morning and was now monopolizing the sofa that Jean-Paul Paul Jean-Pierre had never managed to domesticate, despite the hours and days and weeks he had devoted to it.

Jean-Paul Paul Jean-Pierre was unemployed. He had already worked at and experimented with a myriad of trades, but he didn't really like any of them. Jean-Paul Paul Jean-Pierre liked making things with his hands; he was an artisan but no longer practiced his craft. Jean-Paul Paul Jean-Pierre had never been a good student. Of all his teachers' instructions, of all the numbers and letters in the notebooks, the "immaterial material," as he like to call it, not one bit had stuck in his brain. And he enjoyed believing, was in fact convinced, that such "intellectualities" were not for those of his kind.

Jean-Paul Paul Jean-Pierre was an Indian. You couldn't be any more Indian, outside of India. But he was not a member of the subcontinent's diaspora. He wasn't that kind of Indian. Jean-Paul Paul Jean-Pierre was an American Indian. An autochthonous Aboriginal Indigenous Amerindian and a member of the Great Turtle's North American First Nations. A native of Kitchike. He was born there, lived there, and like his parents before him, got married and divorced there, and then paired up with his neighbour's girlfriend there.

Unlike Jean-Paul Paul Jean-Pierre's parents, the neighbour's girlfriend was not from Kitchike. She was, of course, also an autochthonous Aboriginal Indigenous Amerindian and a member of the Great Turtle's North American First Nations, but she was Algonquin, Anishinaabe. More importantly, she came from the city. The real city, the big city, the City, not the little village next door that the people of Kitchike took for a city. The neighbour's girlfriend didn't know many people in Kitchike. And when the charming neighbour surreptitiously morphed into a nutcase with alcohol-fueled aggressive tendencies, she had simply picked up and moved in with Jean-Paul Paul Jean-Pierre. Since she was there on his sofa, which she seemed unwilling to leave, and since she had no place else to go, he had decided to listen to her grievances and sorrows and to console her. And before he knew it, she'd stayed a while, a night, a year. She had taken up residence in his home, in his mind, and in his heart.

Now, the more he thought about it, the clearer it became. The neighbour's girlfriend, Julie-Frédérique, had settled in, just like that, one fine morning when he'd gotten up, and she'd put down roots in the very sofa where the black hole was now firmly ensconced. Jean-Paul Paul Jean-Pierre wondered if he should bless the cushions for having snagged Julie-Frédérique or scold them for having ensnared the black hole. That piece of furniture was really developing a nasty habit. It had to be subdued, shown who was the boss around there. He had to be respected, but Jean-Paul Paul Jean-Pierre knew nothing about the psychology of sofas. He knew nothing about psychology of any kind. This field of study was not highly developed in Kitchike.

For such services, you had to cross the line, the invisible border separating the reserve from the neighbouring municipality. Jean-Paul Paul Jean-Pierre had spent a long time searching for this dividing line after he'd seen it traced out in red ink on the government's map. And if anyone knew the dusty roads of Old Town inside and out, it was certainly him. Yet he had never been able to find that line of fire, and after having personally witnessed the land surveyors at work, he had determined that such lines were visible only through the specialized telescope used by practitioners of the trade. But it was an instrument that Jean-Paul Paul Jean-Pierre did not know how to play.

Although he didn't know the precise location of the line, Jean-Paul Paul Jean-Pierre, like all of Kitchike's inhabitants, sometimes crossed it to frequent their White neighbours' establishments where they spent the little money they could earn on the reserve. He often earned small amounts here and there, but whatever he earned, he used, as did all of Kitchike's inhabitants, to buy things from his White neighbours. Before he might have said "in the city," as did all of Kitchike's inhabitants, but Julie-Frédérique would have lectured him on that. She had taught him that the city was a different kettle of fish, a fact that went ignored by Kitchike's inhabitants – at least those who did not have the privilege of knowing Julie-Frédérique.

If only she were there.

If only Julie-Frédérique were there, she surely would have known how to get rid of the black hole, which suddenly seemed a little plumper, a little more flamboyant, a little more… well, a little blacker.

But Julie-Frédérique wasn't there.

She had gotten up a little earlier to make her usual female ruckus he was convinced that women were incapable of being discreet and then had left home without uttering a word, as she had done almost every day for the past week, to engage in activities the nature of which she did not reveal. Jean-Paul Paul Jean-Pierre had no idea what he had done to merit the silent treatment, but and of this he was convinced if he wanted to be worthy of recapturing her attention, it would be better for him if the black hole disappeared before she came back.

Jean-Paul Paul Jean-Pierre desperately searched for a solution to his problem. While keeping an eye on the black hole, lest he forget what he was looking for, Jean-Paul Paul Jean-Pierre explored the recesses of his mind. A smile lit up his face for an instant but faded as soon as he realized that he wasn't really looking for the black hole he saw before him but rather for a way to make it go away before Julie-Frédérique returned. Finding that his mind was blank, Jean-Paul Paul Jean-Pierre decided to search his home. Perhaps he'd find an idea in Julie-Frédérique's books.

Since the problem was a black hole, Jean-Paul Paul Jean-Pierre knew perfectly well that the solution had to be contained in the most luminous and colourful of Julie-Frédérique's books. After doing a few turns around the living room, he saw that the most luminous and colourful book wasn't even on Julie-Frédérique's bookshelves; it was right in front of him, next to the black hole on the living room's little glass-topped table, which definitely must not, according to Julie-Frédérique, be mistaken for a footstool.

Jean-Paul Paul Jean-Pierre leaned over, grabbed the book and was set to sit on the sofa but remembered just in time that the seat was already occupied by the black hole. Jean-Paul Paul Jean-Pierre sat on the floor to consult the book whose coloured pages white, yellow, blue and pink held numerous letters and an equal quantity of seven-digit numbers but absolutely nothing concerning black holes. All those numbers did, however, give him an idea. What if he called a specialist from the neighbouring town or rather, one of his White neighbours to help solve the problem? He often earned small amounts here and there, but whatever he earned, he paid out to his White neighbours, among whom he could surely find someone who provided this sort of service. Jean-Paul Paul Jean-Pierre hesitated once again. Should he seek the help of the dog catcher or an exterminator? And really, what was the difference between the two? Not knowing which strategy to adopt, Jean-Paul Paul Jean-Pierre thought it might be better to contact a friend and ask for advice.

Jean-Paul Paul Jean-Pierre didn't have many friends. He did when he was younger, of course. He had myriad acquaintances as well as cousins and relatives whom he could count on the fingers of his feet and the toes of his hands. In his carefully circumscribed universe, everyone knew him, and he knew everyone. His friendliness was the stuff of legend and he was sure everyone appreciated it. In the past, when he was plying his trade, people on the reserve regularly stopped by his workshop to admire his talent. Jean-Paul Paul

Jean-Pierre sometimes wondered why no one came by to see him at his workbench anymore, but then he remembered that even he no longer went there. Some days, Jean-Paul Paul Jean-Pierre wondered why no one called him anymore, but then he remembered that he no longer had a telephone. On other days, Jean-Paul Paul Jean-Pierre wondered why he no longer had a telephone, but then the representatives reminded him that he hadn't paid the bills they'd sent, month after month, until his service had finally been suspended. Sometimes, Jean-Paul Paul Jean-Pierre remembered that he had changed to another telephone company, which bizarrely enough also sent him the same sort of bills, month after month. And this was usually the moment when he remembered that he didn't like bills. It wasn't a question of money but of account management. Jean-Paul Paul Jean-Pierre hated managing anything, not just accounts. He hated managing the food supply, housework, conflicts, and children.

From time to time, Jean-Paul Paul Jean-Pierre wondered why he didn't see his children anymore, why they didn't come to visit him more often. He had four or five kids, who'd moved around according to the seasons, sleeping at his house or his ex's or his mother's or his brother's or his cousin's. Then they'd simply stopped their migrations and settled someplace permanently. Someplace, but not with him. Jean-Paul Paul Jean-Pierre found life simpler that way. It meant he could avoid managing a wide variety of things related to children: conflicts between the kids and Julie-Frédérique about housekeeping, conflicts between the kids and Julie-Frédérique about access to the television or computer, conflicts between the kids and Julie-Frédérique about etiquette, whining and complaining, good table manners, and their curfew. And since he had only the two keys that were included with the new lock Julie-Frédérique had insisted he install before the children ceased their migrations, Jean-Paul Paul Jean-Pierre had determined that this was the indisputable sign of divine will. He was sure of it: destiny had made it so.

In any case, at that precise moment, Jean-Paul Paul Jean-Pierre certainly would have appreciated some help from his offspring. With their children's imagination, they could have helped resolve his nasty black-hole problem. But where were his children? They must be at his mother's or sister's or brother's, or at the home one of his numerous cousins or distant relatives whose names he would probably remember if he ever ran into them, cockade about their neck, at a conference. But Jean-Paul Paul Jean-Pierre never went to conferences. He did however, like the word "cockade." Jean-Paul Paul Jean-Pierre picked up the phone. Well before he found he didn't know whose number he was dialing, he realized that there was no dial tone, although he was sure that Julie-Frédérique had finally found a company that would agree to restore their service. Obviously, he had once again forgotten to pay a bill.

Suddenly, a noise like a wet rawhide strap whipping the air drew him back to the living room, and Jean-Paul Paul Jean-Pierre noticed that he wasn't the only one who had children. Oh, no! No, no, no and no! The black hole, or rather it was becoming clear now the *female* black hole had just given birth to a litter. A huge litter of little black holes that floated here and there, filling his home like so many problems to be handled. And all these problems were swarming and pirouetting through the air and weaving their way into various rooms of his house where they too easily settled on the refrigerator door and in the toilet bowl and in the shower stall and…

Oh, no! Not on the computer keyboard!

If the black hole took the opportunity to browse a website featuring petite Japanese women with generous bosoms, Julie-Frédérique would immediately know and would change the password again, leaving him without internet access for months.

No, no, no and no!

Jean-Paul Paul Jean-Pierre threw himself in front of the computer to block the route of a little black hole, which stopped just centimetres from his face.

"Don't touch that computer!" shouted Jean-Paul Paul Jean-Pierre, imitating the posture Julie-Frédérique took when she scolded him.

"Beat it!"

But the little black hole was more fiendish than he'd thought; so fiendish that it puffed up its belly to raise a multitude of tiny needles as black as the wee black hole's chubby outer layer.

Jean-Paul Paul Jean-Pierre wasn't the faint-hearted type, but he suddenly felt a breeze drift up under his eyelids and cascade all the way down his spine.

The sinister little urchin emitted a strident cry, then began to poke and prick him. Jean-Paul Paul Jean-Pierre dodged it with difficulty, once, twice, then darted under the table to catch his breath. That's when he saw another black hole more voluminous than the little urchin, but not as plump as its mother force open the bedroom door.

"No!"

Jean-Paul Paul Jean-Pierre plucked up his courage and came out of his hiding place. A hail of plates immediately crashed down on him. A few of the little black holes had decided to clean out the cupboards and break everything. Jean-Paul Paul Jean-Pierre ran to the bedroom and found an average-sized black hole snuggled up in bed, on the side where Julie-Frédérique slept, of course. Again, the sound of wet rawhide slashed the air, and Jean-Paul Paul Jean-Pierre saw with horror that this average-sized black hole had delivered yet another litter. There were now hundreds, thousands of black holes buzzing around him and wreaking havoc on his life.

Oh, no! No, no and double-no!

What was Julie-Frédérique going to say this time? He could never handle so much conflict.

A panic-stricken Jean-Paul Paul Jean-Pierre covered his face with one hand and kicked open the front door.

With a swarm of little black holes in hot pursuit, Jean-Paul Paul Jean-Pierre raced to his workshop and took refuge there. There! He was safe now. Beyond the reach of the black holes and their little stingers.

Jean-Paul Paul Jean-Pierre leaned his back against the door and closed his eyes to catch his breath, but he remembered that it was very difficult to pick something up or to pick it up again when you can't see anything. He opened his eyes and, realizing that he still couldn't see very well, groped his way forward to sit on the workbench that he hadn't touched in a donkey's age. Of course, he had no clue who this famous donkey was or if it said donkey was a good-looking animal, a very handsome one, or an esthetically mediocre one his White neighbours seemed to have all kinds but the one thing he knew wholeheartedly was that here, on his favourite of all benches, he was comfortable. He spent a good while in the dim light, studying the tools he'd left lying about, the ash-wood shingle wedges, the basket moulds, the snowshoe frames organized by size on the shelves.

The entire workshop was covered with a thick layer of dust. How long had it been since he'd been here? A week? A month? A year? After his children, his family and his friends, the thing that Jean-Paul Paul Jean-Pierre had loved the most in his little universe carved out with a knife was working with his hands, here at his worktable, reproducing the centuries-old movements of his ancestors.

But Jean-Paul Paul Jean-Pierre no longer plied his trade. How had that happened? He had everything he needed here. He had the time and the talent. And besides, he needed money to spend in the neighbouring town. So why had he given up his vocation?

Jean-Paul Paul Jean-Pierre remembered that the life of an artisan was incompatible with the life of a couple. That dust was bad for his health, that a craftsman didn't make much money, and that he'd be better off finding a real job. He remembered that the smell of rawhide stuck to his skin like glue and extinguished all of Julie-Frédérique's appetite and libido. And that was when Jean-Paul Paul Jean-Pierre remembered that he had simply given up because it was easier to let things slide than to cope with the consequences of his own choices.

Nausea flowed through Jean-Paul Paul Jean-Pierre.

He tried to take a deep breath, but the dust tickled his throat and he began to cough violently. He got up, walked toward the shelving that held the snowshoe frames, stretched his arm out, and grabbed a bottle of beer from his secret stash. He wiped the dust from the bottleneck with the sleeve of his sweater, then uncapped the bottle by striking it against the edge of the counter.

Jean-Paul Paul Jean-Pierre took a long swallow and then a second and a third.

It was obvious that cheap beer didn't age as well as good wine. Jean-Paul Paul Jean-Pierre smashed the empty bottle against the wall. He reached his arm out again, grabbed a second bottle, cleaned the bottleneck, struck it against the counter, and chugged the contents. After completing this ritual a few times, Jean-Paul Paul Jean-Pierre suddenly remembered it had been years since he'd taken a drink and that he'd been all the better for it. Staggering, he sat back down and wondered why he was alone in the dark, doing nothing. Without giving it too much thought, he turned on the light, picked up a basket mould, his racks and other tools, a few ash shingle-wedges, and set about his task.

His nine fingers took on a life of their own, muscle memory doing most of the work. The hours passed, and a few baskets later, Jean-Paul Paul Jean-Pierre realized that he was happy.

It was already dark when Julie-Frédérique burst into the workshop with the full force of her ire.

"What're you doing in here, you big dope? A whole colony of black holes has invaded our house, and you're in here, messing around and wasting your time?"

"I don't know about any black holes," replied Jean-Paul Paul Jean-Pierre. "You can deal with them, since that's your specialty. You know I don't like to handle that sort of thing."

Julie-Frédérique slammed the door behind her.

At dawn, when an exhausted Jean-Paul Paul Jean-Pierre finally went back into the house, he saw that the black holes had disappeared. Then he saw that Julie-Frédérique's computer and her clothes and her underwear and all her books had also disappeared.

Jean-Paul Paul Jean-Pierre fell asleep on his newly vacated sofa as he leafed through the many-hued phonebook, and his dreams were just as colourful.

OMENS

Old Roméo Brokenheart loved the woods that bordered the Kitchike reserve, especially in the spring. On the paths that ran in all directions under the pine and spruce trees, the birch and the maples, he could almost believe that he was, as in his youth, striding across his father's lands in the heart of the Ancestors' territory. Each of his steps made a slight sucking sound. The spongy soil gave off the spicy scent of pine. Here and there, frost still dotted the forest floor. The fresh cool breeze complemented the penetrating heat of the afternoon sun's slanted rays, creating a perfect balance. The air was good. The cracking noises, the earthy odour, the breath of wind on his face, the serenade of the jays, cardinals, and chickadees this was life, real life. Of course, it was an illusion; the reserve, just like the city, was only kilometres away. But since his aging body no longer allowed him to go off on the nomadic adventures of yesteryear, Roméo Brokenheart was content with the woods. He enjoyed each of its sounds and fragrances, every bit of its scenery. It all seemed like a gift to him, a balm soothing his weary spirit. To tell the truth, nothing else could have lightened his mood that day.

Old Roméo sat on a root to consider the brook and the way it sparkled in the spring sunlight. It was a peaceful place. At the advanced age of 76, Roméo could testify to the fact that it hadn't always been this way. In its free-and-easy youth, Kitchike was nothing more than a little hamlet, hardly more than a settlement. Later, houses proliferated almost as quickly as the kids and dogs did. Dusty lanes gave way to paved streets. The packed-earth paths that criss-crossed the community stumbled up against wooden fences with increasing frequency. Roméo didn't understand why members of his race divvied up the space allotted to them or how in their heart of hearts, they could be satisfied with a few square feet of land. Each year, the village devoured more of the woods, which had once been the place where his people lived. It was strange; the more the forest was ceded to urban development, the less it seemed that people went into the woods. The younger generation, hypnotized by the city lights, had slowly but surely abandoned the forest. This had truly saddened the old man, but he found comfort by taking advantage of nature's calm and quiet to gather his thoughts. And today, he would not have appreciated the company of the curious.

Oh! Diane...

The elder let go a sigh that vanished into a little cloud. That was enough to fill him with wonder. The wrinkles on his face lit up.

Sing. It's time to sing.

The old man put his beige canvas sack down and untied the straps. He took out a small hand drum, which unlike his own, was brand new. He took a moment to examine, touch, and smell it. He rubbed it with his palm, making little concentric circles, as if to tame it. Roméo Brokenheart had not yet played this drum. A few years earlier, he had received it as a gift from his great-nephew, a very talented musician who had inherited the Brokenhearts' nomadic spirit. It must be said that Roméo preferred old things, core values that had been proven by experience and the passage of time. But on this morning before leaving, it was this new drum that had called to him and, since his instincts rarely betrayed him, he had decided to give it a chance. The old man rummaged through the pouch that he kept knotted around his neck and took out a pinch of tobacco. He placed the offering on the drum, murmuring the usual prayers. Then he gripped the drumstick in his worn-out fingers and beat a slow rhythm to make the taut skin sing.

Diane, when you were little, this was your song.

You remember, don't you?

Roméo sang. He sang, and each note, each syllable, and each of the words that left his lips joined with the song of Creation, just as tobacco smoke carries prayers. Roméo chanted this song as he had so often done to comfort Diane in their tender youth. Roméo chanted, and in the immaculate blue sky, a roll of thunder worthy of a powerful storm made itself heard. The forest undergrowth stirred. The hares, the partridges, and the squirrels were afraid. Although there were no gusts of wind, everything was on the move.

Roméo grew quiet. He put down the drum and raised his head.

Nothing.

Not a single cloud darkened the sky. Nothing seemed to indicate squalls, heavy rainfall, or storms. Quite the opposite. Even the murmuring of the breeze had ceased.

Oh! Diane, do you remember?

Roméo closed his eyes, the better to see.

A gaping hole appeared in the sky and tore open the roof of the world. And from the highest point in the heavens came a flash of fire, a shooting star that disappeared behind the treetops on the horizon.

Diane, how magnificent it is! How I would love to hold you in my arms right now…

The breeze returned slowly to tickle the nape of old Brokenheart's neck. Curiosity made him scrunch up his face, and he reopened his eyes.

Do you think I could find it again?

In front of him, near the creek, there stood a man. An old friend of the same age. Experience and the passage of time had set them at odds and then separated them. The Cross and the Circle rarely go hand in hand, as both could attest, but it was actually the heart of a woman that had come between them. But today, there he was, here, just as Roméo had seen him in his dream. He was there, here, still the same. He had exchanged the cassock and Roman collar for a plaid jacket and a cap. His back had bent under the weight of the years, and wrinkles had carved their path down his face, which had been lengthened by bitterness. But it was definitely him, Albin Pinault, former missionary of Kitchike.

Roméo put away his drum and uttered a tactless question: "Is the anniversary Mass over?"

The priest did not immediately respond. He lowered his eyes to study his surroundings, spotted a protruding rock, and took a moment to seat himself on it. Still gazing at the creek, he admitted, "I wouldn't know. I didn't have the strength to go."

The man's voice was muffled by pain. He was clearly holding back his tears as well as his words.

Roméo didn't push further. The silence was golden, for both the man of the Circle and the man of the Cross. It was a safe bet, proven by experience and the passage of time. So the two were content to stare at the same stream as it cut through the ice, to be side-by-side as they shared the springtime landscape. They stayed there, here, for a long moment that put down roots.

How much time had passed since their last conversation? How old had Roméo been the last time he'd spoken to Pinault? Sixty, sixty-two? Roméo hated counting the years that way. He considered the custom too linear, too Gregorian. After all, a man matured at his own pace, according to a momentum all his own and at the discretion of the experiences that moulded him. What purpose could such a measurement serve? He had never understood this habit imported from Europe. It was flawed, distorted, and insignificant. Roméo had always believed that the number of years you have left to live would prove to be more relevant than those you've left behind. After all, don't they say that time slips through the hourglass and not that it's added to it? But since no one can predict the amount of time he'll spend on earth, Roméo preferred to ignore candles and birthdays. He had been a child, he'd been a man, and from that point on, he was old, just plain old. Old and terribly alone, left to contend with memories and regrets.

Without looking away from the stream, Roméo scrutinized Albin from the corner of his eye.

The present, you old fool, it is only the present that matters now.

But what words would dare venture into a clearing that had known only silence? Words of tenderness and brotherhood? Or words of war and desolation?

Not knowing which feeling would escape his mouth, Roméo decided to say nothing. He cleared his head by exhaling, one by one, his anxieties and fears in the form of little clouds of steam, then took advantage of each breath of fresh spring air that he could enjoy.

Slowly, the sun disappeared behind the treetops and wove shadows that settled over the two men. But the old friends had already had their share of shadowy darkness and did not want to become lost in it. The subtle diplomacy of the setting sun finally loosened the cleric's tongue.

"If only… if only the investigation hadn't been cut short. If justice had been allowed to follow its course, do you think we'd even be here, five years after the fact?"

"Oh! Albin, come on! You've spent the past 50 years among us. You're practically one of us. Don't you know justice is a dream too heavy to bear in Kitchike? That's asking too much."

"And what about the truth?" murmured Pinault, his voice laced with sobs. "The truth, at least. For her, for Diane. Haven't we suffered enough from this charade?"

"The truth would be nice," agreed Brokenheart in all sincerity. "But like justice, it's hard to find in Kitchike."

"So, all that's left for us is prayer? Prayer and faith?"

Roméo controlled an impulse.

He wanted to reply that faith is all well and good for Christians, that he didn't need it because he had life, the dream, and the Circle. But the weight of grief was already heavy enough for Pinault to bear. And besides, darkness was enveloping the woods.

It was time to go. He stood.

"Follow me. I have something to show you."

Roméo faded into the forest. Surprised but intrigued, the priest rose and followed behind. The two men crept through the falling darkness. Brokenheart led the way, walking as quickly as his aging legs would allow. Albin followed closely after him, even though he struggled to keep the pace. On occasion, Roméo stopped to sniff the air and listen to the night noises, seeking a direction and thus allowing the priest to catch his breath. Albin had no idea where they were going or why his old friend was pushing him into the very heart of the forest. But again today, he had faith in Roméo, despite the distance and the years of silence. Years that accumulated and became a burden, like so many candles on the anniversary of a tragedy. He wondered whether sharing the grief with the eldest of the Brokenhearts would ease the pain of it. Or if it would only rekindle his sense of loss. Whether this damaged friendship could be repaired. Whether that was what Diane would have wanted. Whatever the answer might be, it wouldn't change anything about the fact that he had faith, because faith was what kept him alive. And so he ran. He ran as fast as he could to follow his friend, never managing to close the gap.

Roméo seemed to be in as good shape as he'd been in the past. He ran and ran without tiring. Albin thought for a moment that he was going to lose him in the obscurity of the forest. Then the medicine man stopped at the top of a hill, far ahead, where the moon seemed to shine with a thousand lights.

No, not the moon. Something else. A different celestial body. A warm light that, from the crest of the hill, slipped through the trees and cast shadows in all directions. Hunched over and out of breath, Albin could not stop staring at this light. Intense but gentle. The full luminosity of the star penetrated his body, and a profound serenity permeated the priest right down to his bones. Albin stood back up and then walked forward, solemnly, his step buoyant, as if the pain in his limbs had been relieved by the divine light. And when he finally reached the medicine man, he fell to his knees, joined his hands under his chin and began to pray.

"It's magnificent, isn't it?" asked Roméo, with a blissful smile.

"But… what is it? An angel?"

"It comes from the Sky World. I saw it falling earlier."

The old cleric gazed at the light as if hoping it belonged to him. "Diane…" he pleaded.

"I don't think so, but it's definitely a message," said Roméo, smiling.

Taking one step at a time, Roméo approached the source of light that floated softly in the air. Albin watched it, hesitated, then decided to get up and join the medicine man, close very close to the light source. The light was intense but didn't blind him. Albin felt its gentle warmth envelop him, rock him like a child resting against his mother's breast.

It was, in fact… a little sun.

"How did you know?" asked Albin.

"I dreamt of it. You didn't?"

For a fleeting moment, the old Native's smile became a sneer, though his eyes remained mischievous.

"Méo, you know I don't know anything about that world. What is it?"

"Hope. We may never get justice or truth, but we can have hope."

"Is she sending us a message?"

Brokenheart nodded.

"A gift. A moment to share, just between the two of us."

"Something she never managed to do while she was alive," murmured Albin.

Roméo held out his hand and slowly closed it, one finger at a time, around the little light source, which was immediately extinguished. A subtle glow, a translucent pearl, attached to a braid of sweetgrass throbbed in the palm of his hand. An amulet. Old Roméo turned around and walked awkwardly toward the priest, opened his arms, and gave him an affectionate hug. The two old men stayed there, here, alone in the woods, crying under a discreet moon. And what did it matter if the priest saw it as an angel or a sign from God. For Roméo Brokenheart, it was a light. Made in the image of his little sister Diane, it was a light in the dark of night.

And that was enough for him.

POW-WOW

Jakob Paul spent 10 minutes looking at the portraits of Chief Sacred-Bear that adorned the Band Council's hallway before the muse of all his artistic ambitions ejected the previous visitor from her office. As soon as the chief saw Jakob, he pasted a smile on his face. With an abrupt movement of his left hand, he invited Jakob into his lair.

"Are you still interested in opening up and maintaining the pool?" asked the chief.

"Absolutely," replied Jakob. "Same rate as last year?"

The chief hesitated, grimaced for a moment, and then agreed with a nod of his head.

"I'm warning you right now: This year, I don't want you waiting 'til Saint-Jean-Baptiste Day to open it. I have important guests coming on June 21st. So don't play the Tooktoo with me. Do we understand each other?"

Although he knew how much the current chief hated the Tooktoo family, it was the first time he'd heard that expression. To his mind, it made no more sense than the internecine wars that had raged in Kitchike since the dawn of time. Jakob didn't like the partisan tone the conversation was taking. He wanted to get up and leave the office before the chief's interminable harangue began, but before he knew it, his tongue had already come untied.

"Bah! Shouldn't make such generalizations, Chief Sacred-Bear. Little Sophie who works at the Gas Bar isn't so bad..."

The chief laid his big paw on Jakob's shoulder, keeping him planted in his seat. Sacred-Bear's eyes became dark chasms, and his mouth gaped open. Then he spoke: "A long time ago..."

◎◎◎

A long time ago, big folkloric celebrations used to be held on the Kitchike Indian reserve in the province of Quebec. Back in the day, they were called pow-wows, but they were actually more like costumed sporting events. Every year, all the braves from neighbouring reserves, all the valiant braves from Bersimis, Pointe-Bleue, Village-Huron, and Caughnawaga came running to take part in Chavon Cupcakes' Great Kitchike Pow-Wow. The fastest, strongest, and most skilled men participated in the most prestigious Indian competitions in the province: fox hunting, snowshoe lacing, canoe racing, and of course, seduction of the befeathered young ladies. It must be noted that our girls were absolutely magnificent. I don't know if there's a connection, but at the height of the hippy years, little leather-fringed dresses, Yum Yum-style feathers, and fake black Pocahontas braids attached at the nape of the neck were all the rage. The tan colouring and the short fringes worn as a little loincloth were very "in." We had to conform to the stereotypes that the Whites had assigned to us if we were to attract tourists and put bread and butter on the table. But to be honest, when it came to the young ladies' outfits, the braves did not complain about the show. It was kitsch, but it was *sexy* kitsch. And the girls from the reserve, the spectacular girls from the reserve, loved nothing more than coming to strut their stuff, get worked up, and shout themselves hoarse for the audience of assembled braves.

But in Kitchike, there was a man whose interest the young women did not try to arouse. A man whom they saw but never really noticed: Noé, the long tall string bean with a weak bladder. As legend has it, he could not go 30 minutes without having to pee. It was so bad that he never again drank more than one big glass of water a day in summer scarcely enough to avoid drying up under the reserve's dusty sun. He barely ate anything either, to tell the truth. He had about as much appetite as he had sex appeal. It's not that he was particularly ugly, this Noé. It's rather that his vertiginous verticality seemed to emerge from his socks to reach unimaginable heights, though he appeared to have absolutely no muscle mass whatsoever. The kind of man children throw rocks at when he's not looking. The kind of ready-made victim for Big Chief Tooktoo's disparaging humour.

In any case, that summer, Noé had decided to take his revenge. For once, he would shut that Big Chief Tooktoo's trap. The girls from the reserve the magnificent girls from the reserve, with their faux-braids, real feathers, and their small breasts laced up in leather would come watch, admire, and desire him. Noé would participate in the most prestigious and most impressive of the strongman competitions: the portage race. Now here, I'm not talking about the onshore leg of a canoe race. And I'm not talking about the competition where contestants had to lift a sack of sand strapped to their forehead. No, I'm referring to the prohibited category of extreme sports held in the reserve's backwoods, the great joining of disciplines previously mentioned: the portage race. Strap across the forehead, sack of sand on the back, 200 feet measured from starting line to finish line, a single victor. Because second place is a consolation prize that leaves you all alone to console yourself. There cannot be two Geronimos.

So, like all the assembled braves, Noé limbered up, stretched, had his sandbag weighed. Before taking his place at the starting line, he disappeared into the restroom. No one was surprised: a weak bladder. The braves were getting a little impatient; the public made its irritation known when he returned, but Noé had finally lined up with all the others by the time the starting gun was fired. With 200 pounds on their back and a strap across their forehead, the braves ran and ran along the dirt road, the full length of the prescribed two hundred feet. Contrary to all expectations, the big string bean cut through the wind as if his legs felt none of the weight of his sack. Noé ran and ran. And he won! Noé, the big string bean with a weak bladder, won the qualifying round! The public was flabbergasted. Timidly, then in a more sustained fashion, the bewildered spectators' applause reverberated through the audience.

Then it was time for the semi-finals. Like all the assembled braves, the ones from Bersimis, Pointe-Bleue, Village-Huron, and Caughnawaga, Noé limbered up, stretched, had his sand bag weighed and, before taking his place at the starting line, he once again disappeared into the restroom. Bladder problems. When he returned, he was received with a completely different reaction. The girls from the reserve the magnificent girls from the reserve, with their faux-braids, real feathers, and their small breasts laced up in leather began to cheer for him. For the first time in his life, the big beanpole earned the crowd's acclaim and the sexy kitsch young ladies' war cries. "Noé! Noé! Noé! Woo-woo-woo-woo! Noé! Noé! Noé! Woo-woo-woo-woo!" they shouted, as they slapped their fingers against their pursed lips.

Big fat Chief Tooktoo fired a blank, and the men took to their heels, with the sack strapped to their forehead and sweat running into their butt crack. Four hundred pounds of sand bearing down on a spinal column shod in leather-soled moccasins on a 200-foot-long packed-earth pathway for a string bean from the reserve's backwoods. No less than that. The competitors stumbled behind as a victorious Noé crossed the finish line. The ecstatic crowd leapt to its feet. A few young ladies even unfettered their breasts as if they'd arrived early at a heavy metal concert. For the first time since the event had been invented, a local man was going to the finals! Even the big chief had no choice but to highlight the victory as a turning point in the history of Chavon's Great Kitchike Pow-Wow. Noé was not a member of his family or of his gang or even on his side, but he was a member of his band, and the Big Chief was not going to miss a chance to take a bit of the credit. Fortune favours the bold! Tooktoo hadn't coined the phrase, but he was so cocky that he could have claimed to have done so without cracking a smile.

When it came time for the finals, the spectators in the bleachers bordering the 200-foot-long track were in a frenzy. The residents of Kitchike had spread the word as only the *Kitchikeronon* knew how to do. The place had filled up within a few minutes. The entire community had come to sing the new hero's praises. Tooktoo gave great impassioned speeches in he emphasized the strength, agility, bravery, and perseverance of Kitchike's new favourite son. He confided to the crowd that which he had always greatly admired young Noé, that he had always encouraged him in private, far from the scornful eyes of his peers. Noé was more than his kinsman, more than his role model, he was his brother and the source of his inspiration!

"Noé! Noé! Noé! Woo-woo-woo-woo! Noé! Noé! Noé! Woo-woo-woo-woo!"

Like all the assembled braves, the ones from Bersimis, Pointe-Bleue, Village-Huron, and Caughnawaga, Noé prepared for the grand finale. He limbered up, stretched, had the 650 pounds in his sand bag weighed, and one more time, he disappeared into the restroom.

"Noé! Noé! Noé! Woo-woo-woo-woo! Noé! Noé! Noé! Woo-woo-woo-woo!"

Noé took his place beside the other braves gathered at the starting line, and concentrated on the 200 feet that he had to cover. The big chief called for silence, and then the starting gun was fired. The young braves extended their legs with determined momentum, but Noé was already far ahead of them.

"Noé! Noé! Noé! Woo-woo-woo-woo! Noé! Noé! Noé! Woo-woo-woo-woo!"

Noé ran and ran and ran even faster, as if the weight on his back was growing lighter and lighter. Noé ran and ran and laughed.

"Noé! Noé! Noé! Woo-woo-woo-woo-woo-wooooo!"

The sexy kitsch young ladies' war cries grew lethargic, finally dying out in great befuddlement. Noé ran, ran, and ran. And from his torn bag spilled hay, leaves, and straw… Everything spilled out, absolutely everything but sand!

Noé, the big string bean with a weak bladder, had dared. He had cheated. He had publicly thumbed his nose at the great costumed fair, at the sexy kitsch young ladies who never deigned to look at him, and most of all, at Big Chief Tooktoo, who skulked away in humiliation. And the girls from the reserve and the assembled braves and the crowd from Kitchike and the neighbouring reserves and the Canadian tourists with a taste for something exotic all began to run and run after Noé, who fled laughing.

It wasn't until the next day that they found the sack of sand, the real one, in one of the outhouses.

Thus that was the year that the Kitchike pow-wow lost the sponsorship of Chavon Cupcakes.

⦾⦾⦾

"I don't see where you're trying to go with your story, Chief Sacred-Bear. Is there a moral in there somewhere?"

"You know Noé, that big ole beanpole? He was my uncle. He was the first to dishonour Big Chief Tooktoo. The first to publicly defy him. Some were mad at him because it wasn't easy for us after that. No jobs, no land, no nothing. Pariahs. But me, I looked beyond that. It was the first crack in the tyrannical domination of the Tooktoo clan. That's when I understood that he could fall, that it was possible. It would take me however long it took, decades if necessary, but he was going down. I was going to free us from the Tooktoo's iron yoke, as my father had before me."

Jakob made no comment.

No one liked putting the chief in a bad mood. Perhaps it dated back to the time of Chief Tooktoo. Or of James Sacred-Bear, father of the current chief. Probably even further back, back to the time of the Indian agents, those viceroys crowned by the government and sent to tame the savages. Jakob did not like sermons, or harangues, or big braggarts. But the small contracts that Jack Sacred-Bear offered him improved his finances. Nothing shady: just yard work, snow-plowing, odd jobs. So instead of giving an immoderate response and getting himself into trouble, he chose to keep quiet. Which was no easy task because the chief had this magic power, this shamanistic gift for transforming his words into an invisible finger that poked at your stomach until you vomited up your emotions.

"Nothing to say? Don't tell me you're one of those blind babes-in-the-woods who still believe that Big Tooktoo's reign of terror was even the slightest bit good for our great First Nation?"

"What I think is that you're the chief now, Jack. And that you have the chance to maybe do better than him. And from what you say, that shouldn't be too hard. And right now, since we've agreed about the pool maintenance, I'm going to finish my other little job so I won't fall behind."

Jakob drank his last sip of coffee, plunked his cup on the chief's desk, and then, before going out the door, said goodbye with a nod of his head. No pageantry, no pretence. Simple respect, man to man.

Alone in his office, the chief let out a sigh.

I'm gonna keep an eye on you, you little stinker. I'm gonna keep an eye on you...

MEANWHILE, IN THE NEIGHBOURING TOWN

Meanwhile, in the neighbouring town, Dr. Dentures went to Mr. Meat's shop, where he was surprised to find a long line stretching out in front of the business's little counter. He noticed the crowd's generally dark-skinned complexion, realized that these people were Indians from the reserve, and thought that he recognized several of his clients without being able to identify them by name. No one could really tell one from the other. Despite the appreciable variety of skin tones and hair colours, they were all more or less cut from the same cloth, except for a few squaws who stood out from the others with their willowy forms and refined features. These few pearls, whose beauty almost measured up to that of Canadian women, were few and far between. After scanning the place, Dr. Dentures determined that none were to be found among the fauna that had invaded the butcher shop that morning. Fortunately, Dr. Dentures wasn't the only White in the place.

"Business is good," he confided to Mr. Eyes, who was waiting in front of him. "Not your typical crowd for a Wednesday morning."

"A festival on the reserve, preparations are underway," replied Mr. McClass, who was standing in front of Mr. Eyes.

"Mr. McClass, it seems you've left private education, am I right? Retirement suits you well."

"Too kind, Dr. Dentures, but I prefer to avoid the company of some of my former students, if you know what I mean. I had hoped that Wednesday morning would be prove to be a more civilized time to do my marketing."

"Oh! You know these people as well as I do," replied Mr. Eyes. "They shop any old time at all. They're people with little to keep them busy, other than wetting their whistle," he said, as he mimed taking a little drink.

Mr. McClass and Dr. Dentures laughed so gaily at seeing Mr. Eyes' mimicry that some members of the dark-skinned crowd turned their attention to the two men.

"Shhhh!" sputtered Dr. Scrips, who'd just come in behind Dr. Dentures. "You don't want to get yourselves scalped on your way out, do you?!"

The gentlemen burst out laughing again, a little more heartily this time, provoking immediate silence in the little shop.

"I'm serious," whispered Dr. Scrips. "Think what could happen to your grandchildren in the school yard."

That was enough to sow seeds of doubt in the minds of the men, who resumed their positions and opted for silence.

Thirty minutes later, the place had emptied, and it was the men's turn to be served.

Clearly in a good mood, Mr. Meat pretended to be terribly disappointed, loudly and forcefully proclaiming, "Sorry, but I haven't a morsel of meat left to sell!"

"Nothing at all?" asked Dr. Dentures in surprise.

"Not even a soup bone," confirmed Mr. Meat.

"But that's appalling!" exclaimed the indignant Mr. Eyes. "They left us nothing. They took everything, just like savages!"

"Why don't they go hunt," asked Mr. McClass, "instead of taking the food raised by our farmers?"

"Hah! They're much too lazy!" laughed Dr. Scrips.

"They get preferential treatment!"

"Freeloaders!"

"They pay for all that with our tax money!"

"Stop this nonsense, gentlemen!" objected Mr. Meat. "It's disrespectful, after all."

Mr. Meat stroked the ends of his moustache and waited until his peers had somewhat come back to their senses.

"I don't know where they get their cash," he admitted. "But they pay well, buy when things are on special, and there are no vegetarians on the reserve. My shop wouldn't be the success it is without their patronage. And unless I'm mistaken, your own success depends on them as well."

The four gentlemen hesitated a moment and looked at each other. Then Mr. Eyes exclaimed, "Whatever! They're still freeloaders! They don't even pay for private school!"

"That's not exactly true," said Mr. McClass. "Indian Affairs has been cutting for decades. On the other hand, they still get free dental care!"

"Oh, long gone are the good old days when we were paid per pulled tooth, the better to sell them dentures," said Dr. Dentures. "But the government pays them for as many pairs of glasses as they can break!"

"The funding of optometric services and products certainly proves to be more complicated," said Mr. Eyes, continuing the conversation. "But they don't pay a penny for their medications!"

"Oh, you'd be surprised!" replied Dr. Scrips. "Ottawa slashed the budget ages ago. Since then, we can't foist the most expensive medications off on them. We've had to resort to generics!"

"If I understand well," added Mr. Meat, "these freeloaders aren't so privileged. And the bottom line is that *you* are the ones who truly benefit from Her Majesty's generosity."

Before any of the men could reply, the door squeaked open, and a little Indian entered Mr. Meat's establishment. Dr. Dentures, Mr. Eyes, and Dr. Scrips immediately recognized little Waso, who was – like all of Kitchike's residents – one of their clients. In fact, they didn't so much recognize little Waso as they did the enormous scar that disfigured his face, from his right eye down to his chin.

"Hey, scram!" said Dr. Dentures. "Nothing for you here."

"Mama says she needs chopped meat for Waso's burgers," said the visibly disappointed child.

"Your people took it all so there's nothing left. It's all your fault," said Mr. McClass.

"Not Waso's mama's fault," said the little boy. "She didn't come to Mr. Meat's."

"That's true. Why didn't your mother come to do her own shopping instead of drinking," asked Mr. Eyes, lifting his arm as if to take a drink.

"Mama doesn't drink, she works hard at Gas Bar," replied Waso angrily.

"So Waso will have to go hunt down his chopped meat all by himself," said Dr. Scrips. "A little Indian brave like you should know how to handle a bow and arrow!"

Little Waso's eyes reddened and filled with tears. He turned to leave, but before he went out the door he sadly said,

"Mama says nothing left to hunt in Kitchike. 'Cuz Whites cleared the forest to raise chopped-steak cows."

CHEZ ALPHONSE

Five minutes before noon in the Old Town. A little touch-up to the eye-liner, a quick dash of blush, and a pursing of the mouth to perfect the red lipstick: There, I'm ready to welcome the first of the Sunday clients at Alphonse's Gas Bar. I sit my rear end down on the well-worn stool behind the counter and then wait for the pre-Communion deserters. Every week, the shepherds of the holy flock herald the imminent arrival of devout golden-agers.

as long as the grass shall grow
and as long as the river shall run
after Mass, it's to Alphonse's
that the believer shall go

As if the missionary up on the pulpit so decreed week after week. Which is not the case, as I well know. But it's as if it were true, just the same. I'm not complaining. It's my favourite time of the week. Certainly better than the closing shifts I used to have, when night after night, I had to stand my ground with the drunks trying to weasel one last beer that they couldn't pay for. "I'm gonna pay you for it next week, Lydia," they'd say when I was lucky. When I wasn't so lucky, it was more like, "Can I take it out in trade, Miss Yaskawish?" followed by a hearty, woozy laugh.

Yeah, I prefer the little ladies and gentlemen on their Sunday pilgrimage. Especially when I work with Mrs. Paul.

"And over at Pump Number 2, a ruby-red, double-cab truck, most likely an F150-XLT. Brand new. And inside, we can see... Mrs. Gisèle Wabush!"

Of all the employees, Mrs. Paul has been around the longest. Rumor has it that she was hired by the founder of the Gas Bar himself, the patriarch Alphonse. I think he was the great-grandfather of Max, the current owner who is so cute that half the female employees fall for him. I'm not sure; he died before my mother was born. Alphonse, I mean, not Max. In short, longevity seems to be Mrs. Paul's strong suit. And you don't get loyalty like that anymore. And what's fun with her is that she always has interesting anecdotes about everyone on the reserve. As if each client had his own story, his own universe to be revealed.

"Mrs. Wabush has trusted Ford for her new four-wheeled coach. Congratulations on the new acquisition. We're reminded that her great-grandfather, Simon Wabush, was the first Kitchike native to have a valve-operated car. A magnificent red Tin Lizzie, made by Henry Ford! We immediately see the power of tradition in the Wabush family."

Leaning back against the window, Mrs. Paul gives me the thumbs up to confirm that the game is on. We developed this little routine for when we work together. She settles in near the window, then comments on the arrival of each client, a little like the red carpet at the Oscars. When it's not busy, I play the role of co-host. Time passes more quickly with her.

"Oh! Mrs. Wabush has some competition! Arriving on foot on this beautiful sunny Sunday, it's none other than Jean-Paul Paul Jean-Pierre! The dark shadows on his face and the slump of his shoulders leads us to believe that he has spent another sleepless night."

I crane my neck toward the window to verify this with my own eyes, and I fire back, "His aroma will indicate whether he was on a bender or if he was working the rawhide all night."

Mrs. Paul's eyes light up behind her glasses. Nothing gives her greater pleasure than when I join in. She takes a two-dollar lollipop from the candy counter and brings it to her mouth as if it were a microphone. "To those who might be tempted to believe that his father wanted to play a bad joke on him with such a name, let me remind you that his father bore the name Pierre-Paul Jean-Pierre and, more importantly, that his father before him was named Pierre-Jean Jean-Pierre. But right now, we'd like to congratulate Jean-Paul for having broken the vicious cycle of problematic first names by giving strictly pagan names to his four children!"

With no clients present, we both allow ourselves a good giggle.

Mrs. Paul is in particularly fine form this morning. Poor Jean-Paul. I remember that some time ago, the girls and I had an in-depth discussion of his situation. Since he was one of the only guys from the reserve not having a last name, we'd gotten the bright idea to find him one. Geneviève Sacred-Bear suggested "the man with three first names," but Sophie disagreed. Since two of his names were hyphenated and thus could be de-hyphenated, she claimed that the expression "the man with five first names" would be more accurate. Three slushees and two bags of wavy potato chips later, we agreed on "the man with three to five first names." I don't think the last name stuck. Not surprising, because when you think of it, last names serve, on the one hand, to differentiate, and on the other, to save our saliva.

I hardly had time to greet Jean-Paul before my colleague, from the height of her perch, identified a new arrival: "Ladies and gentlemen, direct from the Church of Saint-Gabriel-de-Kitchike, with her little plaid blouse and her fabulous red-felt vintage hat, literally dating back to the 1940s, it's Mrs. Yvette Sacred-Bear! She is accompanied by her niece Geneviève, with whom I've not had the honour of working for nearly two months. And we congratulate Geneviève on her new but classically styled dress, which she will rarely have an occasion to wear in Kitchike."

I hear Jean-Paul cracking up behind the chips display. Mrs. Paul no longer even tries to be discreet in front of the clients. Seems that as we grow older, we lose that sort of self-control. I take advantage of the time that all this is happening because when the deserters arrive, the rush isn't far behind.

"Your bottles of water, do you sell them in cases?" asks Mrs. Wabush.

Mrs. Paul tells her no. Except for beer, there's no profit to be made selling cases. However, it's certainly the first time that I've seen Mrs. Wabush drinking water.

"Same at my place," says Jean-Paul, who also puts a bottle of water on the counter.

Mrs. Paul doesn't seem to find this abnormal because she proceeds with her show. "Getting out of her used, rust-coloured Sunfire, it's Mrs. Brokenheart, or as the chief would say, 'Jac-que-li-neh!' Fortunately for us, she's made sure to leave her gang of little monsters in the vehicle."

She seems disappointed that I'm not reacting to her most recent announcement, but I'm trying to understand what the deal is with the water bottles.

"An aqueduct problem, I'm sure. The water's brownish, and it smells disgusting," says Mrs. Wabush.

"Definitely going to have to cross the red line and go into town," adds a deadly earnest Jean-Paul.

I never know if he's kidding around or if he's convinced he's said something intelligent.

Mrs. Yvette ends the uneasiness as she sidles up to the counter. She doesn't seem to be displaying her usual zest for life. Her head is so scrunched down between her shoulders that I'm tempted to think that she forgot her neck at Mass. She asks me for her weekly pack of menthol cancer sticks without even looking at me, then hands me the money with a nervous, almost trembling hand. I have enough manners to know not to question an elder, but I nod to Geneviève to signal my curiosity. Before dashing off, Geneviève whispers a few words to me, which I scarcely manage to read on her lips.

"Catherine has disappeared."

Catherine? Catherine who?

It's not like it's the most popular name on the reserve, but just off the top of my head, I can count at least five Catherines. I can't keep myself from feeling a slight shiver. A disappearance is rarely a good thing. When it's a guy, it usually means he's gone to town to squander his pay and that he's had a few cases too many. You know he's coming back. But when it's a girl…

I chase the thought from my mind.

This is no time to let the hamsters run wild, with the convenience store starting to fill up with junkies wanting smokes, gas, and some goodies. Naturally, every arrival is still announced with great fanfare.

"Pierre Wabush has given up his sportswear in favour of a dangerously sexy little black suit. His father was just as sexy during his torrid youth... Mrs. Elizabeth Poker... Wait, I thought that one had gone back to the north. I'm surprised that Madam would stoop so low as to come to Alphonse's!"

I glare at Mrs. Paul. She smiles back like a mischievous child being reprimanded. Max is more patient with her than he is with any other employee, in the name of loyalty and longevity and all, but I'm pretty sure he wouldn't be happy if we insulted his clients.

Pierre comes up to the counter.

Mrs. Paul is right.

He truly is sexy in his suit. I lower my eyes to avoid blushing.

I wouldn't want him to think I'm intimidated because that's not the case.

Pierre Wabush and I have a game of our own. Another kind of game. By day, we are simply acquaintances, we wave to each other or ignore each other. But every once in a while, when we get bored in the evening and we have no one else in our life at the time, we keep each other company. But it's daytime now, so I follow the rules and pay him no heed.

"What's with the invasion of Frogs at the community hall?" he asks, ignoring me as well. "Have you seen that?"

"It's Édouard's gang of Pentecostals," replies Jacqueline. "They invited some French-Canadian pals to their gathering."

"Hah! More reinforcements for their conversion efforts," Pierre fires back. "Watch out, they'll be going door-to-door on the reserve before you know it."

"Hey now, young man. That's not the kind of thing Édouard would do," replies Jacqueline, who is irritated. "Me, I'm more afraid of the swarms of mosquitoes that have invaded the place."

"Yes, it's really weird," says Elizabeth. "A few days ago, it was the rabbits and squirrels fleeing the woods, and today, it's flies! I'm crossing my fingers for the geese."

"Oh! Mosquitoes? That's nothing compared to the invasions of black holes!" says Jean-Paul, nonchalantly crunching on his barbeque potato chips.

You might say he has a way of ending a conversation.

Just as well, because the older folk start streaming in faster than Mrs. Paul can announce them. And that means I no longer have time to play. Within a few minutes, the place has filled up with little ladies happy to be satisfied. I have to smile and be patient, but it doesn't require that much effort. It does me good. I think my little ladies are beautiful. They don't get out often. The Sunday fervour brings them not only the joyfulness of faith but also their weekly share of socializing. Coincidently, it also gives them the chance to show off a new hat or natter about the outfits worn by the less fortunate, whom, they claim, are numerous. Aside from their wrinkles and their groaning, they're a good bunch. I hope to make it there, too. To their age, I mean, not to Mass.

As I'm enjoying the flow of pleasantries and little smiles from the golden-agers, I see Mrs. Paul panicking by the window. I signal to her that I can't leave the cash, but to no avail; she's still getting all worked up and making big signs of the cross.

The Gas Bar's door slowly opens, squeaking like the swinging doors of a western saloon, and the crowd goes silent and remains strangely immobile. The immense man of the cloth, Father Labelle, enters with a clacking of his heels, looking like an elephant in a china shop. As if you'd literally mistaken his stole for a trunk. While his third chin rolls over his clerical collar, his marble gaze comes to rest on each of the customers, studying them one by one with his bulging eyes. The group's level of gaiety goes down a notch. The priest is not happy, that is for sure. And when Father Labelle is not happy, you'd better feel the same way.

"Who?" utter the little lips hidden under the weight of his cheeks. "Who dared?"

No one says a word. No one moves. No one ventures a response because that would be inappropriate. Or because, just like me, no one knows what he is talking about. The silence stretches out for a minute, then another. And long after it has become unbearable, Mrs. Paul remembers that she is working her shift: "Mr. Yvan Labelle, veteran missionary to Congo and inland China, priest of Saint-Gabriel-de-Kitchike! In your presence, the faithful gathered here would like nothing better than to satisfy your thirst for knowledge. If only you could elaborate on the question so that they might understand..."

The older folk hold their breath. The trepidation is palpable. The worshippers stare at Mrs. Paul. How dare she speak to the powerful missionary in that tone of voice? Father Labelle is not the tolerant type. He has been able to instill the fear of God in Kitchike. He is tough and demanding. No one dares raise his eyes when he is giving his sermon. No one complains or criticizes. Barely eight months since he came to the presbytery, and he already has absolute authority. Nothing at all like Father Pinault.

Ever since the former clergyman retired, things haven't been the same. His departure left a gaping hole in the community's religious life. Important to add that Father Pinault spent 50 years with us. He provided his full range of sacraments, from baptism to extreme unction, to three generations of *Kitchikeronon*. We see him again from time to time, but only when there's a death, when he comes to pay his last respects to his adopted community. Always in regular clothes: no more cassock, no more stole, no more Roman collar for Father Pinault. Or rather, for *Mister* Pinault, I should say. Finding a new missionary wasn't easy. You have to understand that priests are like us: an endangered species. In spite of it all, as a mission, Kitchike has an advantage over the neighbouring parishes. The archbishop doesn't want to lose his flock to the traditionalists or worse, to the Pentecostals. So he gives a little more latitude to the mission committee in its choice of clergy. And our elders are demanding. In five years, four priests have come and gone. Kitchike wanted a new Pinault, but it took the mission years to realize that although the person occupying this position wasn't so hard to replace, the man that Father Pinault used to be was irreplaceable. Mrs. Paul says that the committee members should have known this before because the archbishop finally sent them the most zealous of the available priests to satisfy the parish: Labelle. An old missionary who had terrorized neophytes on three continents before returning to the fold, to Canada. As far as I'm concerned, he could have stayed in Africa. I can't abide the fear he instills in my little ladies.

"Well," says the priest as he drags his gargantuan body toward Mrs. Paul. "As requested by the very wise Lorette Paul, queen of the convenience store since the days of Methuselah, I shall clarify my question, using very basic words, as I would in primary school, since this seems to be necessary.

"Just who," he repeated, "who removed Kateri from the church vault?"

The revelation is stupefying enough to set the crowd aflutter. Then panic sets in. The good Christians begin to chatter, offer hypotheses, and accuse each other, primarily those who aren't there. The entire Gas Bar is on the verge of a nervous breakdown. Except me. I heave a sigh as I think over what Geneviève had tried to tell me. "Kateri has disappeared." Not Catherine. *Kateri*.

The statue of Blessed Kateri Tekakwitha, now Saint Kateri, had adorned Saint-Gabriel-de-Kitchike's southern vault since 1984. Rumour was that John Paul II himself had blessed the sculpture during the High Mass he performed for the Indigenous in Sainte-Anne-de-Beaupré. It is the pride of the entire mission, a bit like the mascots of college sports teams in the United States. If there is one unwritten law that everyone in Kitchike knows, it's that you do not touch Kateri. You are free to swear as much as you like, but you do not take the name of the Lily of the Mohawks in vain. And obviously, you do not touch her statue. I have no idea who dared to do such a thing, but he's going to attract more than just the priest's thunder; all of Kitchike's Catholic furor will rain down upon the thief. I can feel it rumbling even here, at Alphonse's. So here I am, powerless to restore order or a good mood on this fine Sunday, my dominical recompense spoiled and my week now definitely starting out on the wrong foot.

Then just when I think the situation can't get any worse, Mrs. Paul yells at the top of her lungs, with all the playful naïveté of a woman in her late 60s, announcing what just might be the highlight of the show: "Alighting from his old grey Mazda with the well-worn paint job, the first date of my life, high priest to the pagans of Kitchike, it's the one and only Roméo Brokenheart!"

Silence falls like a stone. Not another word spoken in the Gas Bar. Aw, damn! That's all we need! My hand reflexively reaches for the phone in case I have to dial 911. I have no idea who the genius was who came up with the expression "things always work out for the best," but he definitely didn't come from Kitchike. Into the midst of the scandal surrounding Kateri's disappearance, into the presence of the bearer of holy terror and his crowd of faithful followers in search of a scapegoat, comes Roméo Brokenheart, the old shaman of Kitchike. My parents, like most Christians of their generation, always told me that he was just an old fool. That he must have a whole gang of ancestral skeletons in his closet and a list of sins longer than he could ever be pardoned for, considering how far from the bell tower of holy truth he had ventured. My opinion is that he's a good person. That's what Mrs. Paul says. In any case, I've never heard him say anything bad about anyone. He always has a nice smile for everyone, a little blissful, a little vacuous sometimes, but he always has a good word for everyone. You can't say that the reverse is true. My little ladies and my little gentlemen have shared plenty of gossip and rumours concerning the malicious Manitou's sidekick, as if Old Méo was the symbol of everything that goes wrong around here. It must be said that over the past 10 years, the church as gradually emptied, and the reserve's traditionalists have been moving up in the world. Several young people abandoned Saint-Gabriel-de-Kitchike and went back to the old ways. The Catholics blame it on Méo the decline of Christian piety, but especially the departure of their beloved priest. I'm sure that deep down, they are aware that the truth lies elsewhere. Pinault had plenty of reasons for leaving. He had led a very full life, and his rest was well-deserved. Plus... there was Diane.

Five years ago, Diane was struck down. In the middle of the night, right here in Kitchike's Old Town. No goodbye, no extreme unction, just a hasty but significant departure. Pinault never got over it. He simply disappeared, as she had, in the middle of the night, leaving a resignation letter at the presbytery. When something like that happens, I imagine that your relationship with God must change, even if you've dedicated your life to Him. Especially if you've dedicated your life to Him. That's what happened with Father Pinault. But obviously no one dared to say it. No one dared to say out loud what everyone knew deep down inside. Because it seems that despite your good deeds, your devotion to the community, and your generosity, when you're married to God and Jesus and the Church, you can't have a girlfriend. Not that kind of girlfriend. It's not allowed; we can't talk about it. We keep it quiet. Even the most wonderful kind of happiness, we keep quiet about it on the reserve. And to fill the silence, we invent all sorts of excuses. Little white lies and dirty little lies. Lies to suit all tastes. Certain wagging tongues claimed that the tragedy was a case of divine retribution because Pinault had traded his position as missionary for the missionary position. Others pointed the finger at Édouard and his gang of Pentecostalists who were developing strong roots on the reserve. But most people considered Roméo Broken-heart to be the perfect source of evil who had driven away their sainted priest. Especially since the two men had been friends in their distant past, before Pinault fell madly in love with Méo's sister. I never understood how you could spout so much nonsense about such a calamity, but that too is just like Kitchike. To hide a truth that is so simple, so noble. That love triumphs, even here, on our minuscule reserve. Even for a priest. Even for an old housekeeper who spent her life celebrating Sainte-Catherine only to finally, belatedly find happiness in the arms of her employer, who just so happened to be a priest.

Old Méo opens the door and enters the Gas Bar, walking slowly as if he were floating in his old moccasins. Despite the silence, the dumbfounded looks, and the very uncharitable whispers coming from the gathering of Catholics, Méo holds his head high and keeps his back straight. He must realize that his presence is causing some turmoil, but he pays it no heed. He greets me with all his wrinkles, gives Mrs. Paul his big, foolish grin and then, as a show of respect, nods his head in the direction of Father Labelle, whose expression remains glacial. Big Méo picks up a copy of the newspaper, puts the exact change on the counter, moves through the crowd, which moves out of his way so that he can plunk himself down at one of the tables at the back of the establishment.

"Lorette, my friend, would you have a pencil to lend me? I think I've lost mine."

"Still with the crosswords, Méo?" answers Mrs. Paul. "Don't you ever get tired of 'em?"

"At our age, it's hard to change our ways."

A few clients take advantage of the brief interruption to pay their bill and leave with their purchases. But the majority remain standing, immobile, facing Father Labelle, who continues his tirade, saying "Someone knows. Even here, in this convenience store, someone knows who stole Kateri. Perhaps the sinner is even in this room!?"

The uncomfortable silence still prevails, but soon several people begin to look back and forth between the priest and the old traditionalist, as if the problem's solution was obvious. A passageway between the priest and the shaman slowly forms in the midst of the crowd, much the same way that the Red Sea was parted by the invisible hand of God. But because Old Méo and the cleric are ignoring the subtle allegations of the faithful, Mrs. Janine, a French-Canadian transplanted from Champlain to live among us, feels free to loudly and clearly express the silent court's verdict: "Father Labelle, you know very well that no Catholic would dare touch our dearly beloved saint. No one would risk his soul for that. The guilty party is surely someone whose soul is dedicated to the flames of the devilish Manitou."

The crowd agrees in a wave of murmurs and head-nodding that crashes up against Old Méo in the back of the room. With his eyes still on his crossword puzzle, the shaman chuckles a bit, then bursts out laughing. Feeling all the eyes in the Gas Bar staring at him, he decides to put his pencil down and raise his head.

"Mrs. Janine, I respect the beliefs of your people and, as a courtesy, I would like you to do the same. Why are you damning me to hell?"

"No one is cursing you," answers Old Hector from the great height of his diminutive five-foot-two-inch frame. "You cursed yourself when you rejected our Saviour and our faith!"

"You cursed yourself from the time you were 20, when you stopped coming to church!" adds Mrs. Janine.

A new wave of murmuring arises, but this time it's more a shower of insults crashing down on the old shaman. Roméo Brokenheart stays calm and composed, the situation fairly comical. As he gazes fixedly at Father Labelle, he replies to the faithful: "Well then, we're in agreement. I haven't set foot in that church for over 50 years, which seems to prove I could not have stolen your Kateri. And since I rejected your Lord and your faith, what on earth would I want with your statue?"

Far from being convinced, the crowd begins to whisper new accusations, listing theories, each one more ridiculous than the next. The frenzy around the priest starts up again. His breathing gets heavier and heavier, his enormous cheeks suffused with blood. One second later, he explodes.

"Enough!" he shouts from deep within his cavernous lungs. "Enough of your useless theories and childish gossiping! Someone knows! Someone must know! Is he going to wait for the divine wrath of God before speaking up? Is he going to wait until the Almighty unleashes the 10 plagues of Egypt on Kitchike? Until water turns to blood, and frogs blanket the reserve, and darkness descends on your homes?"

The priest's rage imposes the silence of the sacristy, a total submission. But when his words enter the minds of the faithful, a new anxiety suddenly disturbs those present.

"The water has already gone bad," says Gisèle Wabush, without truly believing it. "That's why we come buy our water at the Gas Bar, Father."

"And the Frogs have overrun the Pentecostalists meeting," replies Jacqueline in a more serious tone. "Do you think it's a sign?"

"Saint Kateri is at stake here!" exclaims Jean-Paul Paul Jean-Pierre. "The darkness took over my house! Egypt has sent us its plagues!"

Oh, no! Here we go! I feel the fear follow its course before seeing it arrive full force in the eyes of my little gentlemen and my little ladies. The faces become at least three tones of Avon foundation lighter. Mrs. Janine seems to feel unwell; her husband helps her take a seat. Little Hector's eyelids begin to flutter a Morse code, while his click-clacking dentures work hard at shortening his fingernails. The whole Gas Bar is verging on mass hysteria because of a statue's disappearance, and here I am, doing nothing, frozen in place, completely disarmed by the situation. I like my Sunday shift, I like working with Mrs. Paul, I like the old folks, and I like to hear them tell their tales of days gone by. But what I do not like, not one bit, is managing a religious rebellion during my shift.

I try to signal Mrs. Paul, but I can't pick her out in the crowd. She's probably still talking with Méo. I know full well that you don't overcome religious terror through negation, so I decide to push the faithful to the limits of their reasoning to show them their error and, perhaps, surely, I hope, to get rid of that big oaf Labelle.

"Father, can you remind me what the other plagues of Egypt were?"

Labelle takes my question as a challenge. He responds, strutting about to demonstrate to me his mastery of theology: "Wild animals that invade the land, herds that suddenly fall sick, swarms of mosquitoes that cover the earth!"

I regret having opened my mouth as soon as I see the fires of Hell burn even brighter in the eyes of the faithful. I should have kept quiet, as I usually do.

"It's happened!" Janine's husband cries out from the back of the room. "The squirrels and the rabbits have fled the forest!"

"The hordes of insects too! They're here!" adds a small woman whose name I never remember.

"I saw three dead dogs on my way to Mass!" Jacqueline says in conclusion.

I pick up the phone and dial Max's number. It's either the boss or the police, but I don't like the idea of having peace officers disperse a crowd of little old folks because their collective hysteria is interfering with the maintenance of law and order. Plus, depending on which officer is on duty, there is basically a fifty-fifty chance that he'll join in on Labelle's game. The phone rings and rings, and naturally, Max doesn't answer. It's Sunday, so he's at his camp. I raise the hem of my skirt and climb onto the counter to get a better view and to try to spot Mrs. Paul. Once I'm up there, I realize the absurdity of the situation, standing on the Gas Bar's counter in my Sunday best, my little gentlemen and my little ladies terrified at my feet, Mrs. Paul busy flirting with Old Méo at the back of the room, and that little shrimp Herménégilde Wabush ogling my crotch and smiling his toothless grin. It's more than I can take; my nerves get the better of me, and start to yell at the top of my lungs like lunatic.

A moment later, Roméo's voice brings me back to my senses.

"For sure the invasions of bugs and dead dogs, they're scary. Maybe it is the wrath of God, as you say. That, or else it's because of the truckload of rawhide that spilled Friday morning near the shops. Anyway, it stinks like hell through all the plumbing. Lorette, remind me to take a few bottles of water before I leave."

Father Labelle inhales deeply through his nose and seems to hesitate between two actions: hurling himself at Old Méo or making a quick getaway. He chooses the second, then suddenly the terror dissipates, giving way to a deep sense of shame. The crowd shrinks. And as for me, well, I exhale, I resist the urge to plant my shoe in old Wabush's face, and then I climb back down.

The old folks slowly line up to pay their share, at a loss for words and looking dejected. It would be the longest 20 minutes of all my shifts at the Gas Bar – and that even includes Friday evenings – but ultimately the place empties out. Save for Old Méo, still there in the back, doing his crossword puzzles. And Jean-Paul, who was eating his third bag of chips. Ketchup-flavoured, this time.

The rest of the day is particularly tranquil, as are all Sundays. Children come get Slushees and five-cent candies. Two or three tourists fill their gas tanks. A few young people renew their supply of cheap beer to prolong the bender that began two days earlier and end their weekend on a high note. Then just before the end of my shift, I'm treated to a rare visit. So rare that my disbelief makes me shy.

"In his midnight-black SUV, the mission's prodigal son, Mr. Albin Pinault, the pastor emeritus of Kitchike!"

The old priest smiles at me and has a quick chat with Mrs. Paul, but I can clearly see that he doesn't really need anything. The paper bag held his arms seems fairly heavy, and I don't see how he could put any more groceries into it. After a moment, he goes to join Old Méo in the back. I'm stressing out a bit. I have no taste for settling old quarrels between septuagenarians or new religious tensions. But this is not the case. The men greet each other as brothers would, exchange a few words; then the former priest places his bag on the table before leaving, his hands empty and his face serene. Mrs. Paul gives me a long look, her eyes two question marks. Like me, curiosity is gnawing away at her, but she dares not ask. Or rather, she awaits my approval. I nod yes, and then we go join the old traditionalist as if nothing has happened.

"So, Méo, my friend," says Mrs. Paul innocuously, "what did your brother-in-law want?"

Roméo Brokenheart raises his eyes tenderly toward us, hesitates for an instant, then loosens his tongue.

"For me to return his dear Kateri to the fold," he says, indicating the bag on the table. "Albin wanted his blessed saint to intercede on Diane's behalf."

"And he couldn't remember how to get into his own church?" asks Mrs. Paul.

"I think he just didn't have the strength to face his former parishioners. Not with the anniversary Mass. Plus I suppose he didn't want to be asked to explain why he 'borrowed' her to be his replacement. Whatever the reason, I can't be mad at him."

Tomorrow morning at first light, I will crawl on my knees to handsome Max's office and beg him to give me back my night shifts. Bring on the drunkards who ogle my cleavage at the end of the night!

THE CAGE

In the silent freshness of dawn, Elizabeth paused to look one last time at the suitcase lying open on the floor. Everything, absolutely everything was perfect. Each garment had been meticulously folded, juxtaposed to the next, arranged in superb order. Not a single bit of fabric stuck out, not a single protuberance jutted from the stack of garments. In this little universe that she could open and close at will, everything was neat and tidy. Each collar and scarf, each dress and each pair of pants, each of the blouses and tunics, her tights and cotton socks, her brassieres for wilderness camping and nights of drinking, her little panties for virginal days and panties for nights of Bohemian poetry, the reddish-brownish foundation to highlight her prominent cheekbones, the mascara to accentuate the depth of her enigmatic eyes, her toothbrush and hairbrush, every item from her little life was carefully arranged in the glorious receptacle made of purple nylon.

Elizabeth allowed herself a satisfied sigh.

The woman lowered the top of the suitcase and zipped it up with a graceful motion, pausing at each of the four corners, as if offering a humble prayer to the Lord of Nomads. Within a few seconds, she could make the rounds of her portable universe and unpack its secrets, staying for a season or just one night. Then, when the call to migrate made itself heard, she could break camp just as quickly and vanish to new horizons.

Elizabeth raised her eyes for an instant to study the room bathed in the light of the rising sun. Dust swirled through the amber air, and the heat of the sunbeams seemed particularly intense for such an early hour, but all was calm, peaceful. Only the birds singing and the quiet breathing of the man curled up in bed enlivened the soft silence of the moment. Little wooden frames held fairly recent photos that portrayed a few moments of happiness with this man. But like him, these happy times had faded away, leaving room for new dreams and new desires. Elizabeth had understood at a young age that love's magic quickly wore off when faced with the weight of daily life, that it was better to cherish the memories than to get lost in regrets. These few photos had certainly pulled on her heartstrings, but they would not lead her away from her destiny, from her chosen path. True, she had been happy here. One day, when she's old and grey, she'll remember all these wonderful moments and, her heart full of memories, she'll smile. But today, she couldn't allow herself to take anything more than her suitcase with her.

Elizabeth stretched to stand up, but in the middle of her movement, she felt the weight of her choices weighing on her stomach. She had to crouch down for a moment, head lowered, two hands on her suitcase. Her breathing became heavy, and she struggled to maintain control. The cramp lasted only seconds, but the nausea persisted. Her eyes closed, she inhaled deeply, filled her lungs with Kitchike's dusty air, then slowly pressed her navel against her spine to empty them. Gently, she extended her arms like wings and pictured the ocean, the sky, a bird's eye view of the whole universe. Elizabeth breathed deeply as she batted her wings. That was it, she was there. High above, on the roof of the world. Free.

Elizabeth knew the world well. She'd fallen in love with it as a child, during her first trip away from her remote Lower North Shore reserve. Her class had travelled all over France to perform some awkwardly choreographed folk dances. Of all the animals depicted during the show, Elizabeth had been given the role of the Canada goose. To this day, she remained convinced that this was not accidental, that the animal's nomadic spirit recognized itself in her. Ever since, she had sailed on all seven seas, flown over every continent, flitted from island to island, from Réunion to the Isle of Man, from Haiti to the Austral Islands. She had experienced the frantic pace and the deterioration of New York, Paris, and Rio. The sweet tranquility of Huahine and Mauritius. She had been a woman of the world, and every beat of her heart was a call to migration, to flight. Her entire life, an offering to the Lord of Nomads.

Elizabeth stood, and before going through the bedroom door, took one last look at the sublime man sleeping peacefully between the silk sheets. She wanted to whisper through her thin lips one final word, a last "goodbye," a last "thank you," perhaps even an "I love you." But she felt the walls slowly closing in and had to close her eyes to chase away that unwelcome thought.

The trap snapped shut.

It was time to get back on the road.

Now or never.

She grabbed the suitcase and slid it into the hallway leading to the dining room. She could feel her pulse increase as she as she walked faster and faster, but the more she hastened her step, the further away the dining room seemed to be, the more the hallway stretched and lengthened.

She stopped, gripped by panic. At the other end of the hall, the marquetry's inlaid pieces began to vibrate, rise up, and spin about. One by one, they began to fly toward her at breakneck speed. Instinctively, she leapt out of their path and into the living room. She slammed the French doors shut and leaned back against them, gasping. Like a little girl, she had let herself be caught in the trap. Shut away in this house, far from the Lord's gaze, so far from the migratory routes, atrophied in this concrete reserve.

Kitchike.

To Elizabeth, Kitchike was nothing more than a bump in the road, a condition that she had begrudgingly accepted in exchange for some well-deserved tenderness, just to be able to spend a few seasons waking up to this very sedentary man, who had been born there and lived there and would surely die there without ever having seen a thing. But deep in her gut, she knew – she had always known – that this was only one leg of her journey. Moreover, aside from this man, Kitchike did not appeal to her in the least. In her view, it was nothing more than a ghetto full of self-satisfied people. This reserve had neither the tumbledown but authentic charm of her native village nor the stroboscopic attractions of the city. Kitchike was simultaneously too much and not enough. Too close and too far from the city. Not exotic enough but not familiar enough. Too many blue eyes and too much coppery skin. There was no future for her in this place.

She had to hit the road as soon as possible.

Elizabeth dropped her suitcase and pushed the bookcase against the doors as a barricade. She checked the solidity of the window in the living room with her hands, then grabbed a floor lamp to shatter it. The *Food La Bouffe* show filled the TV screen, which came to life of its own accord. Caroline McCann, still round in the belly, was preparing a veal cutlet stuffed with Fontina cheese and prunes. While the television hostess was carefully explaining that her butcher had had to pound the sirloin meat to tenderize it, the lamp's power cord slipped between Elizabeth's legs, and she fell against the sofa, her limbs bound together. Elizabeth flailed around for a moment, but soon her thoughts were caught up in the culinary instructions of the television hostess, who clearly seemed more than happy about her condition. Caroline McCann sliced her French shallots "very finely," while providing the most exhaustive explanations about the next step toward the completion of her stuffed beef cutlets. But well before the chef got to the handling of the prunes, the cries of the Canada geese dotting the ski over Kitchike pulled Elizabeth out of her torpor. Bound from head to toe, she leapt to her feet, broke the mirror above the sofa with a head-butt, grabbed a piece of glass, and cut the cord that was holding her prisoner.

Now freed, Elizabeth hurtled toward the window. She barely had time to glimpse the flight of geese before the metal slats of the venetian blinds closed to block her view. Something was not right. It was spring, so why were the geese going south? She had to get out of there, and quickly. The sweet secret of veal Fontina was going to have to wait.

From the other side of the door, the thrumming of the marquetry had been replaced by the familiar noise of a household appliance. She moved the bookshelf aside, took a furtive glance, and slipped into the corridor, suitcase in hand. That's when Elizabeth realized that the suitcase was much lighter than it had been when she'd entered the living room. Too light. A shiver ran up her spine and settled into her neck. Elizabeth ran toward the bathroom, which was the source of the commotion, and burst through the door. Panic gave way to a sudden surplus of rage. Inside, strewn randomly across the cold floor, was the entire contents of her closet. From the overflowing laundry basket spilled and spread here and there on the ground were every dress and every pair of pants, each of the blouses and tunics, her tights and cotton socks, her brassieres for wilderness camping and nights of drinking, her little panties for virginal days and panties for nights of Bohemian poetry. Virtually everything in her suitcase now lay splayed on the bluish ceramic.

Elizabeth froze for an instant. She couldn't believe it. The whole thing was surreal. She put down the suitcase, unzipped it in three brisk movements, while automatically pausing at each of the four corners, and folded the top back to witness the disaster with her own eyes. The suitcase was empty. Completely empty.

In one swift movement, Elizabeth stood up, went to the vanity, and one by one, opened the bathroom drawers and cupboards, finding there the reddish-brownish foundation to highlight her prominent cheekbones, the mascara to accentuate the depth of her enigmatic eyes, her toothbrush and hairbrush, every item from her little universe that had snuck out of her purple nylon suitcase and cunningly slipped back into the place it was normally kept.

The strident cry that announced the end of the washing machine's cycle rang out through the room. Elizabeth screamed at the top of her lungs, screamed with enough force to break her ribcage. Her yelling set the mirrors and the glass in the windows and shower, and even the bluish ceramic tiles to vibrating. Once she stopped, she heard nothing but the deafening sound of the blood beating against her temples. She took one step toward the machine, then another. With an unsure hand, she raised the washing machine's lid. One at a time, she removed her most beautiful garments. They were soggy but obviously not clean. A quick glance at the nearby dryer revealed that the laundry soap was still in the little measuring cup. She had forgotten the detergent. She had forgotten the detergent and now she had to start the laundry all over again and wait for the end of every cycle of every load, then put each the loads, one at a time, in the dryer, and again wait for her clothes to dry before meticulously folding them up and carefully packing them back into the glorious purple nylon bag. And, once again, she would have to wait for the Lord.

No, she reminded herself. She hadn't forgotten a thing. She had simply packed her little universe in her suitcase in order to leave this goddamn reserve, continue up her journey, and reclaim her nomadic destiny. That was Kitchike. Kitchike, which forced her to put down roots, to exchange the thrill of flight for the routine of a sedentary life with no horizon, to watch the seasons pass by instead of dancing with them.

No, she thought again. She would not let herself be deterred so easily.

Elizabeth threw herself to the floor and began to repack her suitcase, as quickly as she could. She grabbed the clothes scattered on the floor, the ones in the basket, even the wet ones in the washing machine, and she crammed them into the glorious purple nylon bag.

As the suitcase gradually swallowed up the fabrics, the laundry basket at her side gradually regurgitated them. She redoubled her efforts, trying to be quicker than the basket, which was refilling itself and spitting back every dress and every pair of pants, each of the blouses and tunics, her tights and cotton socks, her brassieres for wilderness camping and nights of drinking, her little panties for virginal days and panties for nights of Bohemian poetry.

The lid of the washing machine came down, and Elizabeth heard the stream of water refilling the tub. She stopped, defeated. She was fighting a losing battle. She would never leave this world with her cherished possessions. If she wanted to leave this house, this concrete reserve, she'd have to do it the way her nomadic ancestors from Nutshimit did it, with a minimum of baggage.

A powerful gust blew against the bathroom window. Elizabeth glanced at it. A great blizzard was roaring across a thick white carpet, violently shaking the few trees that were somehow resisting the storm. Winter. Winter had arrived so early that year. The cold crept its way into her belly, and she felt her legs trembling. Again, Elizabeth bent her back, closed her eyes, and exhaled. She raised her arms like wings and tried to lift her spirit above the soft white carpet. But she didn't know how to fly in a storm, how to orient herself in the blizzard. The glacial wind froze her bones, and her spirit had to come back down to earth.

Elizabeth opened her eyes.

With slow but determined steps, she left the room and went back to the dining room adjacent to the entryway. This time, the hallway did not try to hold her back. She removed a key from her keyring. Put it on the island. Hesitated a moment in front of the closet. Thought of how the cycle of seasons had picked up its pace. Finally chose a spring coat. Purple, like the suitcase left behind. She put it on. Touched her fingers to the doorknob. Hesitated again. Then turned the handle to open the door.

And just as she was finally preparing to become master of her destiny again, a noise held her back. A cry, pure and fragile, but as powerful as the unleashing of the seasons. A cry that snuck in through her ears and travelled down into her gut where it tied her stomach in knots, then ran the length of her legs, making her unsteady on her feet. A cry made in her image, fragile and despairing: a newborn's whimper. The weight of the world dropped to her belly, and once again she felt the vice tightening its on grip her.

She withdrew her hand from the doorknob. Turned her head. The claws. She started to walk down the hallway that she'd had such difficulty leaving and went to the back, all the way to the back of the little room across from the bedroom where she'd left that sedentary man asleep, the man with whom she'd shared a few moments of happiness, moments that she would treasure one day when she was old, so old that she'd have nothing left but these tender memories to cherish.

The door was wide open. Inside the little room and bathed in light from the rising sun were a changing table, a cradle, tiny moccasins, and little dreamcatcher with pastel-coloured feathers attached to the window. The amber air was filled with dust motes, but everything was calm, peaceful. Elizabeth's enigmatic eyes widened. The nausea, the cramps, the indecisions, the resistance against the migratory call… Kitchike was no longer trying to hold her back; it already held her through her womb.

The door to the room closed of its own accord.

Once again, Elizabeth felt the walls closing in on her. But this time, she would not bow down, or stretch out her arms to withdraw into her dreams of freedom. She would fight as a warrior and a survivor, forced to be sedentary but remaining wild and free. A powerful anger rose up and set her ablaze. Elizabeth raised her head and opened her mouth to spit out a roaring fire. She howled, and her flames engulfed the little room. She screamed hard enough to burst her lungs and tear her vocal cords. She screamed, and her cry grew longer, louder, more powerful; it spread and filled the room, until she was hoarse and panting… And when the cry died out, the flames had carried away all the little furniture, the entirety of this little world. Everything had disappeared, save for the marquetry on the floor, which was now covered with thick dust. Everything had fallen victim to the flames or the ravages of time.

Elizabeth slowly turned toward the door and met her own eyes in the mirror hanging on the wall. She instantly recognized the old wooden mirror, which had once belonged to her grandparents. She also recognized the resigned, exhausted look in her eyes. But the rest of the image did not suit her. Her face was covered in wrinkles, her silvery-white hair was coarse and hung loose on her old, stooped shoulders. Her sagging breasts hung over her enormous belly, which in turn hung over her belt. She no longer recognized herself. This was all that was left of her. She had been sucked in, harnessed to a life she had never wanted.

Through the partially open window, she heard the birds calling her. She scanned the sky and saw a flight of geese returning from the south. They had left without her but returned to greet her. Elizabeth's heart grew heavy. The bedroom door creaked open. A tiny girl in pink pyjamas toddled toward her, a stuffed toy in her hand. She wasn't more than four years old. She stared worriedly at Elizabeth for a moment and then asked, "Gammy, why you yell? Wha' happen to you?"

Elizabeth took a step forward, picked the little one up in her arms and hugged her fiercely. She whispered, "Kitchike, my beautiful Victoria. Kitchike is what happened to me."

"Gammy, we going to feed the birds?" asked the little girl, who pointed to the flock of geese in the garden.

"Not those, Victoria. They would forget to leave."

Elizabeth cried all the rains of the new season, never knowing whether she shed tears of sorrow or tears of joy.

ZOMBIE

Today's not the day that the sky will lift its veil of darkness. That's not going to happen any time soon. I should have done what everyone else did and made sure I took a goddamn umbrella with me before I left. Then I would've avoided this uncomfortable feeling of dampness that's followed me all the way into the belly of the beast. But I won't bother anyone. I'm not here to make friends. I have a feeling I won't be here long enough for that.

I had just entered the establishment when the doorman buttonholed me and demanded my ID. For real? I celebrated my 40th birthday a few years ago. Maybe these days there's a maximum age for getting into this kind of club. The burly guy in the velvet sweat-jacket assured me that that wasn't the case. Just a random check on newcomers.

"We don't want any trouble here," he stated in a tone that was half-aggressive, half-blasé.

I winked at him in an effort to be reassuring. He inspected my driver's license a little longer than necessary, then went on to clarify his thinking. "Pierre Wabush, huh? We're not used to seeing Indian braves dressed up in silk."

Some would take offence at the comment's subtle racism, but I decided to maintain my stoic attitude.

I came to the Halloway strictly for business. I'm not keen on this kind of place: post-gothic hall, haunted by pretentious snots made up to look like raccoons. Vampires who beg for their peers' attention, overreacting to anything and everything. You'd think you were in a period piece. Not too sure which one because I never really was very good in history, especially so-called "European" history. The sort of period when people spoke of themselves in the third person. The sort of period when people hid their hypocrisy under a thick layer of romanticism. The smell of rat, with the floral scent of decay. The sort of period when women encased themselves in a wasp-waist corset under their brassiere, then hid their teeth with a fan to mask breath that smelled like a maggoty toad's. Wait, now that I think about it, I wonder why they didn't just use their hand, the way the girls on the reserve do to hide their teeth when they giggle in public. Probably because back then, Whites had chapped hands. That would explain why the women wore little white lace gloves. In any case, here, you might believe you were in that kind of mad, mad world. The same, only remixed by Rob Zombie. Because everything is black, everything is decorated with a pseudo-gloomy look that exudes a melancholy straight out of *Twilight*.

The bar is adorned with twittering gargoyles, both on the walls and on the dance floor. The wooden furniture is decorated with humanoid skulls, and the heads of does, oxen, bucks, wolves, and even freakin' chickens (I guess they have something against turtles and bears because I didn't see any of those). The heavy metal music is playing with its usual subtleties, making the lighting gear tremble. I have neither the patience nor the short-term memory necessary for counting the number of fake, made-in-China LED lanterns lined up on the tables and behind the counter. It's depressing, even without considering the local fauna: somewhat effeminate men with long, straightened hair and dyed eyebrows, draped in dark clothing to make themselves look austere. Loose women tattooed like the Devil, covered in lace from petticoat to hat, their breasts thrust toward curious eyes by push-up bras. And they've all lightened their skin to look deader than Dracula.

Everything is fake. Absolutely everything.

This is not my kind of place nor is this sort of crowd that impresses me.

No, me, I come from Kitchike's Old Town. I'm used to seeing under-educated little punks acting all noble when it comes to landing a job. Back-of-the-reserve lowlifes take themselves for tie-wearing big shots as soon as they get the big job or a great deal, or worse, win their fucking election.

I can smell fakery from a mile away.

Nevertheless, I try to act at ease in this nest of nutcases. I try not to look too pissed off. To melt into the jungle, to act all casual as usual. This requires a bit of subtlety when I raise my eyes toward the inverted-crucifix clock above the counter-cum-sacrificial altar. It's a lot harder to contain my consternation when I note that their "little Jesus" is sporting an erection. Whoa! I know a ton of people back home who'd turn that into a whole scandal, but I don't have time to pay any more attention to it because just then the barmaid comes toward me with her slutty smile. Her bosom is so heavy that it risks tearing the lace at the buttonholes of her blouse. She must have tired tits.

"How can I be of service, kind sir?" she says as she makes a polite little curtsey.

Kind sir. Yeah, right.

You must look quite the gentleman wearing this clown costume, a black suit with a puffy-collared white shirt. It'd be an outfit for a buffoon even if it wasn't soaked through and through. You don't just feel like a wet duck, you feel like a lame duck.

Ha! A gentleman, for sure. Shit.

But anyway, I resist the urge to say that yes, in fact she actually could help me by accompanying me back to my room, that I feel a terrible ache in my soul that only an attentive woman could cure, but only temporarily.

I don't want her to fall in love with me because as soon as I get what I came here to get, I'm going back to my no man's land of a reserve.

Oh! Excuse me! I'm not being politically correct. Now, one must say "my First Nation's territory." I don't know which idiot replaced the word "reserve" with "First Nation." Because on the one hand, a nation is not a territory, it's a people. And a community is not a people in and of itself. At this point, there as many nations as there are villages. And on top of that, they're all called "first" so no one's feathers get ruffled when they're numbered, like the old treaties that the British authorities shoved up our ass – *sans* lubricant – one after the other.

Not us, obviously. Not Kitchike.

As for us, we had no right to numbers because we'd already been fucked by the French. And 400 years later, we still have their dick stuck down our throat while the British screw us from the other end. That's us. Kitchike, MILF of the oldest colonial gang bang the earth has ever seen. There's a good reason why we dare not retaliate, that we allow ourselves to be bribed by any poster boy with an iron fist who runs for election.

The waitress seems confused.

I suppose that that's what you get when you ask someone a simple question, and she stares vacantly at you, lost in her thoughts. At least if I'd stared at her chest, so beautifully enhanced by her seductive attire, she would have understood.

Not happening: zombie mode.

"Sir?"

Okay, Wabush, save face, just to avoid upsetting her, then maybe, yes, maybe you'll earn the right to a little "motherly" kindness.

I plunge my eyes into the deep valley that forms between the cups of her bra and answer, "I'll have a Grand Marnier. Double. On ice."

She smiles and nods, one eyelid heavier than the other, then disappears into the little crowd of uptight prigs, her hips swaying. Perhaps her wink meant to convey a message. After all, if you judge by the surroundings, she must not be accustomed to seeing burly dark-skinned guys. It's not that you're particularly good-looking, Wabush, but if you compared yourself to the wimps and cockroaches crawling about here, you'd probably get picked for a TV reality show.

The waitress moves off, and my eyes follow her long legs encased in black, mid-thigh fishnet stockings, climb up her mini-skirt, stop at her ample buttocks for an instant, then track the length of her bare back, and finally delicately land on the cross bearing the Antichrist (who has a hard-on, just like me) that serves as a clock.

Five minutes to midnight.

My contact should be arriving any minute now. He might already be here.

I move closer to the counter, the better to observe the macabre fauna. I sweep my eyes around the place, gawking actually, and taking care to linger on the young ladies' cleavages and derrières. This allows me to conceal the true purpose of my "scrutination" (I know it's not a real word, but I honestly don't give a shit) while I enjoy the landscape. No harm in mixing work and pleasure as long as you don't forget which one takes precedence.

A mauve scarf. That's the only indication I was given. The only clue to help me identify my contact in this nest of worms. A fucking mauve scarf. Why not a gold tooth while we're at it?

I couldn't identify a monkey wearing skates in here, with the schizophrenic semi-darkness broken up by strobe lights. Especially since the place is beginning to fill up at this hour, the time when ghosts come out. Fortunately, mauve doesn't seem to be this crowd's favourite colour. My eyes are drying up from all my "scrutination" (yes, still at it). I finally detect a few fragments of mauve floating around the edge of the dance floor. I approach discreetly, while signalling to the waitress so she won't have to look for me.

A few steps in the right direction and I realize that it's a woman. A pretty, plump redhead with full lips. Fuck, this is going to take forever. I'm pretty sure that my contact is supposed to be a man, so I stop in my tracks. I'm not the kind of guy people notice. Not the kind of guy who gets propositioned in a bar by young ladies who are all smiles as they waggle their rear end like a she-cat in heat. I prefer Kitchike's open houses. I prefer to go incognito. Still, I must admit that every once in a while, I tell myself that a bit of belly-bumping with a little White female would do me the greatest good. I'm obviously talking about a woman, not a polar bear cub.

I don't have much experience with hips. They're not common on the reserves. My old buddy Jakob once told me that there's nothing hotter than getting a little White woman down on all fours and taking her from behind, while you steer her hips like a Formula 1 driver, and then giving her the old joystick until you come. I take one more look at the little redhead wiggling her hips to the beat of the neogothic howlers providing the so-called music in this dump and decide that I wouldn't mind trying out *her* steering wheel. A guy could get a good grip; seems she has the right stuff in the right places. And at the same time, I thank the Lord for the prevailing darkness that hides the bump swelling up in my shorts.

The waitress brings me my double, which I sip more quickly than I would have hoped. I exchange a few platitudes, just enough to get a smile, and when I look again at the dance floor, I realize that the redhead has disappeared. Or rather, that she has gracefully settled onto her perch, alone at a table. I hadn't taken two steps in her direction when she turned and pierced me with her big, soul-devouring eyes. Big green eyes like the hope that you should never have. I froze, mortified. For an instant. Or two or three or four, I'm not sure, but I know that the very next second I get an elbow in the ribs and find myself face to face with the spitting image of The Rock all six-five, six-six of him and before I know it, my shoes and the bottom of my shorts double in size, because I suddenly lose all control.

"Forget it, pal. Laura, she's the boss's old lady. Steer clear."

I nod to let him know that I've caught on, but to avoid being too polite, I clear my throat at the same time.

I understand you, but I couldn't care less.

I do not care in the least about the boss. Come to think of it, I don't give a damn about Laura and all that. Don't give a damn about little White women, whether they're redhaired or blond or brown-haired or as green as the hope you must never have. Big jerk of a fairy, thinks he's Lou Ferrigno. No harm in looking, is there, eh? I'm here on business, eh? I remind myself so as not to forget because sometimes, it's hard to remember those kinds of things when you're getting shafted. I gulp down the rest of the liquid and swallow the ice cubes so I don't burn my throat. Yeah. Fuck.

"Eggplant!"

The push-up bra hands me another Grand Marnier. I barely have time to pay for it before I order another. I gulp down three-quarters of it and then realize that it's blazing hot in this friggin' furnace. A little wink, a good tip, I restrain the hand that feels like patting the waitress's ass as a way of thanking her, then once I buck up my courage, I finally make up my mind to go sit with Laura, who is nonchalantly wriggling around on her chair, and damn if I wouldn't take her right there on that very seat, with her leaning on her elbows, breasts all squeezed together, and mouth half-open. In that order, or a different one. Provided that I could get my hands on the steering wheel. The world is a circle, so fuck the little Jesus with his boner who's been telling me the same fucking thing since I came in here.

Five minutes to midnight at the Halloway.

Fuck that and good evening, sweetheart!

"Sweetheart? Not very original, my tall-dark-and-handsome man," Laura's luscious lips countered.

At least, I assume that it's her lips that are answering me because I can't see anything more than that. I realize that I'm there, sitting beside her, inhaling her pheromones from a little too close, a little too roguishly, my big leg warming itself against her burning-hot thigh…

I push away my sixth drink. Far from me, all the way to the other end of the little wooden table adorned with the head of a stag, his antlers tall and imperious, with a reproachful look on his face. Fuck that. I've already had enough of the crucifix mocking me with its zone of temporal relativism, without having the representative of the Council of Animals watching over me, faces looking all holier-than-thou. I never was the religious type. The pillars of tradition always disgusted me as much as the pillars of the church did. Don't do this, don't do that… acting all superior, with their fucking rectitude… it's not as if it's ever saved anyone.

"In any case, certainly not you!" says the alcohol, even as it warms the back of my throat.

I sigh into Laura's neck. Her piercing look goes straight into the very depths of my soul; I feel the hair stand up on the back of my neck, and then everywhere else too.

Focus, Wabush! That's not what you came here for, for God's sake!

I jump up and head to the washroom. I do so with disconcerting rapidity, considering my partially pickled state. As I'm going into the john, I'm bumped by an innocent young queer à la Edward Cullen who doesn't seem to be walking any straighter than I am.

"Hey! Zombie, pay attention or you'll mess up your hairdo!" I say as I take a quick look in the mirror.

"Judge all you want, but at least me and my guys have our eyes open and a heart that pumps blood. You're the only one here who looks like a zombie."

He slams the door and leaves me alone with my frustrations and prejudices. Alone in front of the damn sink. I rinse my face with unsteady hands, and the truth catches up with me. Fucking big slacker who shoves ideas into your brain. But he's right about one thing. Vampires radiate thrills and excitement while you wear your grey like a day of remembrance.

You're just passing through, Wabush. That's obvious here, but don't start thinking it's any different on the fucking reserve. You were six years old, and you left one school for another. Passing through dark streets, after-hours bars, and open houses. Anywhere you can drink other people's beer. In Lydia's bed, and Sophie's, and even Jakob's, on the days when he deigns to go to work and leaves his lady friend home alone. Passing through assignments to "project work," as they call employment integration programs in the village. Like most people on the reserve, you're a zombie who's passing through. A zombie who shuts his trap and watches time pass while self-righteous phonies and the big shots of our zucchini republics (have you ever seen a banana growing on a reserve?) feather their nests with federal grants and give family members every available job, from the most prestigious to the most insignificant. A goddamn zombie, yeah. Not wrong. He's not wrong, that fucking Whitey. But that doesn't give him the right to put on haughty airs like some shitty colonizer.

I'm gonna show them! I'm gonna put what Jakob says about women to the test. Not his woman; I already tried, and she doesn't have the right steering mechanism. Nah, tonight, it's gonna be Laura's hips. I'm gonna tie her hands together with her friggin' mauve scarf and make her moan until she forks over the little photos I came here to get. Fuck, yeah!

To enhance my smile, I dry my teeth, making sure I have no surprises stuck in between them. I fluff my hair, smooth down my eyebrows. Voilà. He's ready, he's back: the predator of Kitchike, released incognito into the bowels of the big city.

The Grand Marnier suddenly inspires me to try a classic move from the *Karate Kid* (the original, of course), even though I probably look more like some kind of fucking flamingo; I slowly raise my right leg while trying to balance on my left. I let loose with a shriek that's meant to be a war cry, then kick the door open to go back into the halo of light surrounding the lovely Laura. And then…

I don't know if I miscalculated my distances, but the hallway unexpectedly shrinks up, and I find myself on my ass in the damp cold of a dark alley, catapulted outward through a very well-placed service door. This is no accident; I'm pretty sure I'm not the first person this has happened to here, but I don't give a damn. Because all of a sudden, the halos of the streetlights begin to flicker just like the bar's strobe lights, and I'm being hammered with big punches delivered to the beat of techno-gothic bass guitars muffled by the brick facade. The music ends with a crescendo of blows to the gut – left-right, left-right-jab! And a kick in the teeth for the grand finale.

Bloody hell. If I hadn't been so drunk, I think I would've passed out.

Fuck that.

"I warned you not to go near the boss's old lady, big chief. I don't wanna see you around here again," growls the Dwayne Johnson lookalike.

Half comatose, I see the gorilla disappear through the service door. Lying on the asphalt in the foetal position, bathing in my own pool of blood – and, parenthetically, of vomit – I note that the rain has finally let up at the wrong moment. It might have helped me clean myself off. Then just as I'm I thinking that I did all this for nothing, that I'm going to go back to Kitchike empty-handed like a fucking loser, I hear footsteps.

I twist around for a second so that I can sit up and lean against the wall and wait for the continuation of my drubbing. In my present state, there's no question of running, no question of defending myself. And I'm fairly certain that I have a few teeth left to brush. To my greatest surprise, it's the man in the sweat-jacket coming toward me. The same big doofus who carded me at the entrance to the Halloway. I notice his beautiful leather shoes for the first time. My impulse is to warn him not to walk in the puddle of blood, but I contain myself. He can very well muck around in the shit just like me.

"Sorry about the stratagem, Geronimo. It was my best idea for how to do this incognito."

I was going to congratulate him on his clever use of a word like "stratagem," but reality was getting a little fuzzier. Out of nowhere, without warning, he drops a brown envelope, too close to the puddle of rain-blood-vomit for my taste. I quickly grab it and slip it into my pants, as if my entire life depended on that damn envelope. At that point, I realize that the combination of Grand Marnier and an alleyway beating had done its work because I don't understand anything anymore.

The guy lights up a cigarette and asks, "Not that it's any of my business, but what exactly did he do to you?"

I mask my discomfort by puffing out my chest. I tap the bottom of my pack of cigarettes to extract a cancer stick. Then I give him the side-eye, à la Tarantino, presenting him with my hooked-nose-Injun profile.

"You're right, it's none of your business."

He lets out a bitter little laugh. Then a big one. The sweat-jacketed dumbass seems to find the situation rather amusing. At the end of the day, I have to admit that if the roles were reversed, I'd be laughing just as hard. I let out a brief round of chuckles and end with a deeply felt "fuck you." He looks serious again.

"You want to make him sing? I'm not new to this business."

"I don't want anything from that guy. I'm doing it for the cash, just like you."

The White dude in the sweat jacket looks disappointed. He clearly sees that I'm lying to him. That I hate the Big Chief the way reserve dogs hate pickup trucks. I'm transparent, even at the bottom of this alleyway, toothless and practically comatose. I don't know if it's just to be polite or if he couldn't care less or if it's just to hammer the nail deeper into my brain, but he throws my suppositions back in my face: "What makes you say that? That I'm just in it for the money?"

I must confess that he surprises me, and it must show on my face. Oddly, it never occurred to me that this fucking White dude might have motivations other than the cash. And no, not just because he's White. I simply assumed that anyone willing to risk his life to stand up to the people in the little photos and come deliver them in this demented hole in the wall and to a total stranger, to a savage, no less, must be the lowest level of vermin out looking for money to treat himself to a torrid night with the young ladies or other such foolishness.

Suddenly, I have to know.

"So why do you do it?" I hiss through my teeth.

"Who knows? Maybe for the thrill. To spice up my life a bit. Or maybe I'm just a good soldier."

This time, I'm the one who laughs. Not too hard and not too long because it kills my stomach and everything else that the alcoholic anesthesia hadn't properly numbed.

"Good soldiers aren't curious. They obey orders and don't ask questions."

He comes closer, takes a puff of his cigarette, bends his knees to come down to my level, and coughs a lungful of smoke in my face.

"Maybe it's simpler than you think. Maybe I find it entertaining to watch you devouring each other like dogs."

He holds his pose for a moment, eyes squinting, lips tight. I think that he's trying to intimidate me by playing the cowboy. As if! Pure trickery. Smoke and mirrors. Maybe I'd fall for it if he showed even the slightest mastery of his game, but such is not the case. I say maybe, but the truth is, maybe not. Because in the end, it wouldn't change a single thing. You don't need a goddamn sweat jacket to sow the seeds of discord. The storm has been raging on the reserve since they passed the sacred and inviolable *Indian Act* over a century ago. Bloody little White guy with a Napoleon complex, who likes to pretend he's James Bond to prove to himself that he's good for more than just carding the redskins who come to his fucking den of imbeciles.

Fuck that!

This guy has nothing against us. No, it's his own employer that he's mad at. Good for him if he wants to wear a sweat jacket and act like he's on *The Sopranos*; he's small-time. A flunky for the bigwigs who pull the strings. It's the serviceable Indian who doesn't even have the luxury of being Indian. And

I bet he'd like it as much as I would if the faces in the photos appeared on every channel and on every screen. I must admit that that one, I didn't see it coming.

Once again, I burst out laughing. I let rip a big, liberating guffaw even though I'm spitting up all the blood in my pain-wracked lungs. I laugh so hard that my bones rattle. I stare into his little second-rate-actor eyes, and I get it off my chest.

He wants to know why? He's gonna know why.

The truth. The whole truth and nothing but the truth, your Honour!

"The truth is that big old Sacred-Bear didn't do anything to me. Absolutely nothing, never and under no circumstances. Nothing bad, nothing good. He never took me seriously, never waved hello. But I've seen everything he does in Kitchike. How he enjoys playing the Good Lord with the life of everyone on the reserve. How he meddles in absolutely everything so that every day he amasses a little more power, more control, more cash, more privileges. And I never said a word.

"Like the rest of the gang of zombies, I pretended I didn't see a thing while he filled his pockets. I saw him get rid of three executive directors and half the band's managers for refusing to cover up his scams and swindles. I saw him trap the chief of police with accusations of trafficking coke when the guy wanted to stop his son-in-law who was driving drunk the night that Brokenheart got hit. I was a passive witness when he started cutting the salaries of minor officials so that he could continue to support the lawyers and consultants who finance his elections.

"When he doesn't need those guys for major claims, he uses them to shut up his opponents by dragging them to court for defamation. None of it keeps him from jetting off to every continent to let everyone know how pitiful we are.

"And worst of all, the straw that broke the camel's back that was already broken: he closed the elementary school midterm for lack of funds, just as he was giving a start-up grant to his own business! No more, goddamn it, no more!

"A photo of him looking like the grand prince of Canada is plastered all over the reserve. And no one has the guts to stand up to this goddamn bandit. In our fucked-up communist regime of a republic run by brainless fools, people know that if they want a house, a loan, a job, hunting grounds, a vaccination, an hour at the ballpark, a kiosk at the pow-wow, or just to be able to rent the community hall for their daughter's wedding, they have to keep their mouth shut. Worse yet, they have to sing the same song as Sacred-Bear, in tune and at the same tempo, even if they don't know the words. Good goddamn, NO MORE!"

The man in the sweat jacket drops his cigarette into the puddle of water and takes his time to slowly exhale the smoke accumulated in his lungs. Before ducking out, he confesses: "You're right, Geronimo. In the end, I want exactly the same thing as you."

I suppose there aren't that many differences between the way you manage a reserve, a business, or organized crime. It's all the same. A bit like the golden days of the "Europes." You hide your hypocrisy under a thick layer of romanticism. The smell of rat, with perfume to cover the rancid odour. The truth is that perhaps we've all been corrupted to our very soul, if such a thing exists.

I stub out my cigarette, and then I leave too.

I go back to the hotel, my dick hard as a stag's, my head full of lace bra cups, my teeth loose, and my hands dirty. I should have done what they do in period films and put on little white gloves. I'm going to sleep poorly tonight. But tomorrow...

Tomorrow, Wabush, you'll be back on your fucking reserve, the little photos in your pocket, but you won't be the little canary who's ready to sing.

Fuck you, Big Chief.

THE MAN WHO MAKES THE STARS DANCE

Yawendara hadn't come for the music. She was there for the young man, the one on the poster. For him, and the secret that was his. She gingerly raises the cup and takes a sip of her blueberry tisane. Lukewarm. She'd been waiting a while. Still, waiting didn't bother her. Hidden within the crowd, the young woman took a certain pleasure in observing the artist, who had just come on stage. The young man's hair was smooth and twisted into two long braids that hung on either side of his face. He was sporting a bowler hat decorated with a silver brooch and a few dyed-red turkey feathers. Below the hat, his features were rugged and severe. His aquiline nose dominated thin lips. He seemed young. No more than 18, 19 at the most.

The Wampum Café was a tranquil place. A small performance space located on the outskirts of Kitchike, a hangout for the reserve's poets, eccentrics, and art lovers, plus the Indian-lovers from the neighbouring town. Good food, adequate coffee, excellent beer at an acceptable price. Tasteful neo-indigenous décor for those who didn't care to wallow in lowbrow folklore. It was definitely the community's hottest spot, a fact that, according to its critics, meant little considering the notable absence of any competition. In any case, the establishment occasionally presented shows of a more than decent calibre. That night, the establishment was welcoming a young guitar virtuoso. On the wall, a colour poster announced him as being *Teandishru', the man who makes the stars dance*. The young man had performed at the country's various Indigenous festivals and was returning home, triumphant, to complete his tour in front of an audience he'd already won over, some 50 people gathered together between the room's stone walls.

After a few words by way of introduction—. "Thanks for coming out in such great numbers" and "It's such a pleasure to play in my hometown tonight" and other little white lies and obligatory clichés – he finally began his performance. Seated on his little wooden stool, Teandishru' skillfully slid his fingers along the strings to elicit some lively and stirring sonorities. No, Yawendara had not come for the music, but the music came to her. Like the rest of the audience, she was soon engulfed by the exquisite notes that flooded her ears in a succession of exhilarating waves. The splendour of the melody transported her elsewhere, far away, to that serene space that borders the different states of consciousness. Far away, yes, but not far enough.

The musician's small, slightly slanted eyes burned with an unbridled passion that emerged with each new note. Under the shower of bluish light that pierced the room's shadows, Yawendara no longer saw the performer, but someone possessed, exalted. The music was certainly more than just a job for Teandishru'. It was nourishment, a vital essence that bewitched him and that he cherished in the deepest part of his being. The young man abandoned himself to the melodies and allowed himself to be consumed by his unity with his guitar, which enabled him to create a whole new universe in the time it took to play one piece. The young woman had never seen such a fusion between a man and his instrument. The music transformed the young man into a celestial being, an intangible *oki*, a purity of rhythms and vibrations, of beauty and power. Yawendara was hypnotized by the performance. Time seemed to stand still, the pieces following one after the other in a symphonic dream from which one never wanted to awaken.

Still sitting with her hands resting on her thighs, her chin held high, Yawendara was no longer there. Her spirit roamed through the luminous void of transcendence, dancing from one sphere to the next. High above, her essence tried to identify the contents of different universes by examining their outer membranes, having known for a long time that the content such spheres was made in the image of the container, a simple tridimensional projection of a space-time limited to two dimensions. But she could not linger long enough over each universe to find the one that was home because the cosmic dance kept leading her higher and higher into the zones of consciousness.

While the hands of Teandishru' lingered on the last note of the last piece, applause spread through the room. Drained, Yawendara opened her eyes. She was once again trapped in Kitchike. Gone astray. Exiled. Lost. The mystical force that had been before the crowd had disappeared: There was only Teandishru', a young man who now had none of the charisma he'd had a moment earlier. Yawendara remembered that she wasn't there for the music. She let out a heavy sigh. The time for introductions had come.

⊚⊚⊚

Dog-tired but ecstatic, Teandishru' collapsed on the sofa in his dressing room. A towel around his neck, the man undid a few buttons on his shirt, then closed his eyes for a moment. The audience had appreciated his performance. For the third time that week, he'd filled the room. It's true that this was not a great achievement in and of itself: The Wampum Café had scarcely more that 50 seats. Still, he was satisfied. No, he was proud. Proud and confident in the future. The night before, the establishment's manager had told the young musician that an agent from a big hall out West had attended his show and had been deeply moved and touched his performance. Teandishru' could already picture himself on that prestigious institution's stage. According to the manager, only the most promising artists performed there, which was enough to inspire the dreams of any musician working in a poorly paying environment. Teandishru' had a brilliant future ahead of him, and he knew it. He could visualize it, feel it, almost touch the dream he carried inside.

A strange odour drew him out of his reveries. A spicy, fruity perfume suddenly caressed his nostrils. Teandishru' opened his eyes and turned around. Standing near his makeup table was a young woman. She seemed to be a few years younger than him, probably 16 or 17 years old. The young woman's beauty was enough to inspire the greatest melodies. Her straight hair, cut to shoulder length, was a deep black, as were her eyes. She wore a dark velvet dress decorated with various buttons and embroidered with whorls of flowers, probably sewn with moose or horse hair. She had fine facial features. Looking at her, you might have believed that the beauty of all Creation was nothing but a hymn composed in her honour. Surprised and seduced, Teandishru' was hypnotized by this vision. Although he was too tired for the lightning bolt of love, he certainly felt the thunder rumbling within.

"The man who makes the stars dance," the young woman said, with a touch of irony. "I thought you'd be taller. And older. You can't believe the hype."

Teandishru' realized that he was staring at her, dumbstruck. And that she had just spoken to him.

"You work here?"

The young woman said not a word. She just smiled, shaking her head back and forth to say no.

"Are you interested in my music?"

She burst out laughing like a young girl, which in fact she almost was.

Teandishru' felt the insecurity tighten around his neck.

"You have no reason to be here!" he said, cutting her short as he rose from the couch. "This dressing room is reserved for artists and their invited guests."

"Oh, I was invited, Teandishru'. You invited me," she explained, with an air of mystery.

For some reason, this timeless beauty was now giving him goosebumps. Her eyes, while sparkling, made him shiver, as if a mystical aura enveloped the young woman. He hesitated, resisted the urge to call security for a moment, then gave a sigh of resignation.

"I'm really tired. I'm going to ask you to leave. Otherwise, I..."

The woman's face darkened. It didn't exactly turn nasty, just stony.

"You won't get rid of me with threats. In another time, when I was but a child, I faced stone giants. I survived a horde of the living dead. I made it through the mazes in the Forest of Severed Heads and faced off against the Son-of-Agreskwe. So childish threats do not impress me much."

"Hey! I'm 19 years old, and I'm certainly older than you are! Are you also going to tell me you fought the flying-heads with your bare hands? That you were transformed into a giant bear to confront a man-eating willow tree? I suppose that your name is *Yawendara*? We're not in a kids' story here!"

"No," replied the dark and brooding young woman. "Anyway, as for the flying-heads and the man-eating willow, you're right: that never happened. But as for the rest, it's all true. And I *am* Yawendara."

Was she serious or was this just a bad joke? The mother of Teandishru' was originally from Wendake. He had spent several years of his childhood there. *Yawendara and the Forest of the Severed Heads* was part of the Grade 6 curriculum. He vaguely remembered the novel's twists and turns, as well as the other adventures he and his friends had had to invent for an assignment. Never, even in his childhood reveries, had he believed that the main character could spring to life and come knock on his door. Or rather, surreptitiously sneak into his dressing room. The situation was being determined either by a more than dubious sense of humour or by a relatively severe case of schizophrenia. The musician tended to favour the first option because the second presented a different question: which of the two was actually suffering from it?

"I know about *Hansel and Gretel*, too," added Teandishru'. "Tell me, are you related?"

"I don't think so," said Yawendara. "I didn't come here to talk about those far-distant times. I came for you. I have questions, and I'm staying until I hear the answers."

Teandishru' observed her for a long moment, desperately seeking a way to get rid of her without making a scene. Her silence continued, and he could no longer stand the young woman's steady gaze. He was worn out, and his hunger gnawed at him. He gave in. Perhaps she was crazy, but she didn't seem dangerous. And besides, she was quite nice to look at.

He sighed.

"Okay, meet me over on the bistro side."

◎◎◎

After showering and changing, the young musician joined Yawendara in the restaurant. Its menu was limited, but on weekends, the kitchen was open until 11:00. And it served the best *sagamité* in the entire province, something that he would never tell his mother for fear of antagonizing her.

Yawendara's sharp eyes analyzed the artist. The young man was arrogant and sure of himself. The charisma he exuded on stage had completely melted away. She could almost believe this was an entirely different person.

"So? What impelled you to sneak into my dressing room and hold me prisoner?" he asked jokingly.

Yawendara smiled and replied, "The amulet that the old man gave you. A glass bead attached to a chain of sweetgrass. It belongs to me."

Teandishru' was about to swallow another spoonful of his thick, corn-based soup but stopped the utensil midway between the bowl and his mouth. He raised an eyebrow.

"The amulet?' he exclaimed in astonishment. "You came to me about some tacky piece of jewelry?"

"Precisely! I was passing near here, and I felt something... something strong, powerful. Some instinct pulled me toward your reality. I came closer, and when I was looking through the membrane between our two worlds, I saw the old man give you *my* amulet!"

Drip by drip, the soup Teandishru' hadn't had a chance to swallow fell from his mouth. He slowly closed his jaw, chewed the few bits of remaining meat, and swallowed with difficulty.

Yawendara seemed oblivious to the totally nonsensical nature of her words. Surely there was something else. How could she know that his uncle had given him a necklace? How could she describe it so perfectly?

"Are you spying on me?" he asked defiantly.

"Of course not. I know that the old man found my amulet and that he decided to give it to you. He probably saw something in you. Your music is powerful. There must be a medicine man in your family for you to be such a powerful *oki*."

Teandishru' froze. He scratched nervously at the paper placemat. His annoyance had given way to a heavy, gripping fear. He had no idea how this young woman, who also claimed to be the character from a book he'd read as a child, knew so many things about him. It wasn't real. It couldn't be real. He must be dreaming, that was it. Exhausted, he must have fallen asleep in his dressing room and was in the middle of a dream. The waitress brought him out of his stupor: "A little bread here? A piece of bannock?"

His eyes were still fixed on Yawendara; he sent the waitress away with a wave of his hand. Then he exclaimed, "Are you even real?"

"Of course! If only you weren't so superstitious, with your simplistic materialism, you would understand."

"Whoa! A character from a fairy tale is calling *me* superstitious?"

"You're the one talking about fairy tales. I am Yawendara. If your world has nothing of me but a simple echo, it's possible that I inspired a storyteller, a writer, or even better, what do you call them? A filmmaker. The fact remains that I am extremely real."

Faced with the perplexed scepticism of Teandishru', Yawendara held out her hand, as if trying to prove her point once and for all. She insisted with a nod of her head. The musician obeyed. Slowly at first and then more vigorously, he squeezed her palm, then her whole hand.

"Ouch! I wanted you to touch me, not tear off a finger!"

"Sorry."

"So, can we agree that I'm real?"

He nodded, still just as flabbergasted. To tell the truth, Teandishru' was no longer sure of anything.

"You say that you're Wendat," Yawendara spoke again.

"My mother is."

"Your mother, right. From where I come from, if your mother..."

"I'm *Kitchikeronon*."

"Don't know what that is. No matter. If you're Onkwehonwe, a descendent of the Original Peoples, you must know that what we can see with our eyes is only a tiny part of reality."

"Lovely superstitions," the musician retorted.

"I'm talking about science! With every breath of the Multiverse, new realities erupt and are born into the original fire. Would it be so surprising if my deep imprint was broadcast on more than one frequency? It's just that here, there's only an echo of me. I come from elsewhere, another world, better organized than it is here, more beautiful, freer and so, so..."

"We really should have you committed."

"But I'm only a fictional character, sprung from an author's imagination, what could anyone hold against me?"

This was too much for the young musician. His head was spinning, and the bile rose in his throat. He had to end this conversation as quickly as possible. And run, far away from this young beauty who was messing with his mind.

Teandishru' picked up his bag, felt around the bottom for a minute, and took out the amulet that his great-uncle Roméo had given him. As if a lightning bolt had shattered the darkness of a stormy sky, the Wampum Café dining room was suddenly pierced by a brief burst of intense light. Teandishru' didn't move. He'd had the pendant for a few days, but never had he seen it shine so brightly.

Yawendara gave no sign of surprise.

She extended her hand, grabbed the amulet, and held it between her palms to diminish its radiance.

The young woman fastened the delicate braid of sweetgrass around her neck, then hid the gem under her dress. Her dark pupils shone with a thousand lights. With one movement that seemed to last an eternity, her delicate eyelids tenderly closed over them. A smile formed on her face, which had never seemed so beautiful. A tear slid down the length of her lashes and then dropped, falling slowly, slowly, toward her bowl of soup. When it finally reached the broth, a deep, muted sound was heard. A shock wave ran through the room, creating a bubble of immobility that caught and held everyone frozen in place.

Everyone except Yawendara and the musician.

"And now, Teandishru'? You think you're more real than me? And these customers, that waitress? You still think that your whole world is more real than mine?"

The young man's eyes scanned the room, briefly studying each of the customers sitting motionless in the sound bubble, as if they were merely actors in a film that had been put on pause. In fact, nothing seemed real anymore.

Teandishru' realized that he was no longer panicking.

The comforting warmth of Yawendara's amulet had alleviated the fear that had invaded the deepest part of his being. The young woman's troubling revelations no longer frightened him. Quite the contrary. Teandishru' felt peaceful once again, the way he felt when he abandoned himself to music.

He was surprised to find himself thinking about his grandfather. A memory, a specific and distinct feeling. He was only five years old, on a night with a full moon, near a sacred fire, the red-hot rocks drenched with cedar water. The comforting warmth of the lodge. That's what he felt at that precise moment, in that bubble vibrating with a deep sound. And as he did when he was a child, he allowed himself to have second thoughts. About the world around him and its rules, about everything he'd learned and everything he'd presumed to be true. And suddenly, the world seemed new and marvelous. The world was offering him a dizzying number of possibilities. So many questions were jostling about inside his mind. He didn't know where to begin, so he took a leap of faith and relied on the young woman, as he had with his grandfather so long ago.

"I have no idea where to start," he admitted. "What question should I ask to get you to answer me honestly? Is it… allowed?"

"Many things should not be allowed," replied Yawendara. "My presence here, for example. But you read about me, so you must know that that never stopped me. Not when my entire being is convinced that my motivations and my actions are just and honorable. Besides, your world intrigues me. Your village, your nation…"

"What are you trying to say? My village, my little universe, the place where I was raised…"

"That doesn't exist where I come from. Nor in any other universe that I can see. At first, I thought it was a bad joke. And anyway, what language does the name 'Kitchike' come from? What does it mean?"

"I don't know," said the musician. "I don't speak my language."

"Does someone here know?"

"It's an old word. No one remembers."

"I speak at least seven languages, and I can assure you that the word doesn't come from any of them that I know well. Seems that it's a made-up word. Artificial. 'Kitchi-' sounds Algonquian. In Atikamekw or Cree, it means powerful. The 'ke' ending is a locative suffix in the Iroquois languages. It means 'the place where this thing is found.'"

"What are you suggesting? That my nation doesn't exist? That we were created out of thin air… like you?"

"The Wendats exist in most of the universes I've been able to observe. In several, our civilization has spread beyond the solar system!"

"So, am I supposed to feel reassured, knowing that I'm at least half real?" grumbled the musician.

"Teandishru', I'm not trying to insult you, or upset or antagonize you. But only by achieving a deep awareness will you be able to find your true path."

Teandishru' lost his nerve for a moment as he tried to grasp the full scope of Yawendara's words. If he followed her logic – if some kind of logic could be found in what she'd said – then was he nothing but a member of the Malamek nation? And Kitchike, just another Kinogamish? As in *Wulustek*, the play by Dave Jenniss. Or as in *Mesnak*, Sioui Durand's film. Was his entire world just the simple result of an essentialization process used to address the overall status of Indigenous peoples in a fictional drama? As impossible as it might seem, he suddenly found the idea alluring, possible, true.

"You see," Yawendara told him gently, "your world is not any more real than mine. Not in its present form. It's just… a low-resolution representation of a different reality. Distorted, malleable, sculpted on the basis of an echo originating elsewhere, probably actualized through a process of individual creation. It's very common. More so than you might think."

"You mean to say that I'm also a complete fabrication? That I'm the product of some author's imagination?"

"At least that's what I believed. But when I heard you play earlier and witnessed your power; I began to wonder. The process may be more reciprocal than I thought."

"Now you've lost me again!"

"What if it's the reverse?" Yawendara continued. "If the breadth of our exhibitionist impulses and our unhealthy need for attention was combined with our desire to believe in something greater than us... And what if we were the ones who invented our creators and our public? Just to feel less alone. Just to have the impression that our life has meaning for someone, somewhere?"

Still enclosed in the calm vibrating bubble, warmed by Yawendara's soft solar aura, the musician took the time to think about each of the young woman's words.

The silence went on a little longer, pulsing at the same rhythm as the sphere of timelessness. For the first time, Teandishru' clearly understood Yawendara's uncertainty. A question burned on his lips, but he already knew the answer. "You're not supposed to be here, are you?"

The young woman hesitated and squirmed in her chair for a moment before sitting up straight again. She gave a small shrug of her shoulders and then admitted, "Definitely not. I should be back home, in my universe."

"So why aren't you? Why did your amulet end up here with me? Why were you... unmoored?"

The young woman broke down and wept. Her tears spilled in a rush that flooded the soup, and at the same time broke the bubble of immobility.

All around them, the customers and the staff came back to life as if nothing had ever happened.

Teandishru' was startled.

Yawendara didn't seem to notice. Through her sobs, she told him everything, everything she'd seen in a dream.

"There was an irregularity. My spirit was captured, torn from my reality, then broadcast on every frequency. Since then, my Creator has cried day and night. As if his soul had been taken over. He stopped eating and let himself go. He lived as a recluse, a hermit, like a Robinson Crusoe, a tramp, an oddity. I have to find him. Make things right. Stop this pain. I want to go back up to my Creator's universe to dry his tears."

The musician listened to her without reacting, without commenting. She appeared to be so fragile, so human, so pure. The crowds waiting for him out West mattered little, the career he might aspire to here mattered little, the dreams he'd been able to treasure a few hours earlier mattered little. He saw that all of it was nothing more than an illusion. All that counted now was right before him. All that counted was the truth as it was revealed through this young woman's lips. And all that he wanted, in his heart of hearts, was to know the elation of joining her in her quest.

"That's why you need the power of the amulet that Little Turtle gave you?" asked Teandishru', recalling the novel from his childhood.

"No, the amulet is only a compass. To travel in the upper regions of consciousness, all I need is power. All I need is you," she said, drying the last of her tears. "Are you coming?"

⊙⊙⊙

Before a bonfire, somewhere in Kitchike's woods, Teandishru' sat on the ground, guitar in hand, and began to make his instrument sing. Perhaps he was the creation of someone else's imagination, but he too was an artist, a creator. And it was this realization that changed absolutely everything for him. No, he was not just a puppet. He was an actor, someone who worked in a divine burrow, an intersection of roots uniting the lifetimes of a single tree. He could now see the system into which he was woven; he could free himself of his chains and soar to higher levels of consciousness. And more importantly, he could take on his true role: navigating the infinite and exploring all its possibilities, all the histories, all the stories arising from the primordial fire.

"And what about the legends? All the stories that have been passed down to us for centuries and have no authors?"

"I don't know. Maybe they're from more permanent worlds, from stable, self-sufficient universes that don't need a creator to sustain them. Because they are found at the top of the consciousness hierarchy… My head's about to explode! Are you ready?"

If the musician had been invented by characters hungry for attention, he was grateful to them. It was time for him to leave the place of his birth and generate currents to new worlds, where he could draw the contour of his readers and, more importantly, of his Creator. He believed this with all his heart:

There lay his destiny. But he suddenly realized that he didn't know how to navigate through these lands. He stopped strumming his instrument and stood up.

"Wait, before we go, tell me how it works when we leave a bubble-universe?"

"Don't worry about the take-off. But watch out for the landing. Once you've broken through an opening in the roof of a world, you'll find yourself in free-fall."

Yawendara tied her hair back in a ponytail and then pulled the amulet out from under her dress. Teandishru' closed his eyes and surrendered himself to his guitar. The incandescent jewel glowed brighter and brighter with each new note the musician played. The little sun's light joined with that of the fire, and soon the two young people were completely bathed in light.

"What do I do to survive the fall?"

"You have to have faith, Teandishru'. You have to believe."

"In what? In you?"

The young woman smiled and teased, "No, believe that you can make the stars dance!"

And the melodious light erased them from this sphere of existence and transported them to the heart of the primordial soup.

In the little universe of Kitchike, they were never seen again. Some claimed that they'd fled to the west and lost their soul in the Downtown Eastside. Others maintained that Teandishru' had converted and stopped making his guitar sing. The Elders, who understood the Pleiades' lament, knew something else to be true.

They said that the pair was living happily, in the place where all realities exist, and that there, they were sowing the seeds of thousands of children throughout all time.

THE HARD FALL

With his big, damp mitts, Chief Sacred-Bear replaced the glasses that annoyance and sweat had caused to slide down to the end of his nose. Once again, he inspected the photos that had appeared on his desk. He saw the exact same thing he'd seen the first dozen times. His business dinner at the ranch. Himself, the Banker, the Investor, the Lawyer, and the other. The other, whose name must not be spoken. All the people directly or indirectly involved in the recrew-tourism megaproject at Poste-au-Chien-Blanc. Difreddi. Shit, now he'd said it. Difreddi.

"Jac-que-li-neh!" the chief yelled at the top of his lungs. His secretary obligingly hurried into his sumptuous office, coffee in hand.

She was nervous, more agitated than usual, but Chief Sacred-Bear failed to notice.

"Finally," he said, handing her a piece of paper. "Now, dear Jac-que-li-neh, our reaction time is limited. If you still want to have food to feed your four little runts at the end of the day, I suggest that you be so kind as to summon each one of the pricks on this list. And in this order. I want them here this morning, obviously, because when the media descend upon us, there will be no tomorrow."

I

Jakob the Rascal calmly showed up 15 minutes after receiving Jacqueline's phone call. It must be said that he had neither regular work nor a passion to delay him, neither at home nor anywhere else, so when the chief called for him, he might have assumed that perhaps there would be a little job for him or at least a spicy anecdote for him to sink his teeth into. And this anecdote, Jakob had heard when he stopped at the Chez Alphonse Gas Bar on his way to the Council offices. He promptly realized that it was more cartilaginous lump than savoury morsel, the kind of anecdote you can easily choke on and die, but since he wouldn't be the one doing the choking, he decided to enter the chief's office with his habitually mild amiability, which managed to irritate Sacred-Bear even more.

"What's the feeling out there? What're people saying at the Gas Bar? Can we keep the damages to a minimum?"

"Everyone knows, Chief Sacred-Bear. It took me exactly 15 minutes to get here, and I'm sure even the dogs are spreading the word. Plus, if we were anywhere else, there'd probably be an angry mob in front of the Band Council, demanding your resignation."

"But what else?"

"Since we're in Kitchike, I guess people are just going to gossip while they patiently wait for the Quebec cops to arrive or for the minister to throw you out of your seat by decree."

"And you think that's funny? That makes you happy, you little scalawag?"

"I can't say that it makes me particularly happy. But yes, I find it fairly amusing that you've spent your first mandate complaining about your predecessor's shady deals, and here you get caught during your second one. You can't be mad at me; irony is all we have around here to liven things up. And for that, I must thank you."

"Who is it? Who did it? You're such a busybody, you must have some idea!"

"I don't know anyone on the reserve who's in contact with that gang, Chief Sacred-Bear. Aside from you, of course, which I was unaware of until yesterday. I actually thought you were going to clear all this up for me."

"If I knew, I wouldn't need you!" shouted the chief as he unknotted his tie.

"Okay, Okay! Don't stress out! So, about the maintenance of your swimming pool, I'd be happy to keep taking care of it even while you're in prison. Same rate for the next three years, but at a certain point, we'll have to calculate for inflation..."

"Get lost!" hollered Sacred-Bear, his face red as a chili pepper.

And indeed, Jakob the Rascal complied, and departed in haste.

II

The Lawyer answered through his secretary that, unfortunately, he could neither meet nor represent Chief Sacred-Bear due to an apparent conflict of interest, but he strongly recommended another member of his firm, thus making the chief angrier than Jacqueline would have believed possible.

After futilely invoking the name of each of the 12 apostles and of Canada's eight martyred saints, and even that of the beatified and now sainted Kateri Tekakwitha, he decided fairly abruptly and unilaterally to break all business connections with the firm that had, however, financed each of his electoral campaigns by declaring that if his "old friend" wasn't coming to the trial as legal counsel, he would be there as his accomplice. Sacred-Bear was relatively certain that he'd hung up faster than the nitwit at the other end of the line, but just to be sure, he picked up the receiver and banged it against the phone set, hollering out the name of his Saviour in a rather unchristian manner.

III

The Investor was a former schoolmaster from the neighbouring town and was both unmarried and childless. Newly retired, he had developed the habit over several years of diversifying his sources of income by investing his nest egg in various, more or less reputable companies. Numerous business opportunities had been offered to him by one of his former students, a prestidigitator from the reserve who was particularly skilled with the magic of numbers, especially the art of making them disappear and reappear at just the right time. And it was through this Indian (which, according to him, he was, but in name only) that the Investor had met Chief Sacred-Bear. Since then, he had met said chief a few times at the ranch or at La Cité, but to avoid raising suspicions, never on the reserve or in the neighbouring town. In addition, it was with dreadful irritation that he received Sacred-Bear's demand to appear at his offices without delay.

The Investor hung up the telephone, swallowed his last bit of croissant, returned the jar of jam to the refrigerator, and carefully rinsed his dishes and utensils in lukewarm water. He took off his shirt to brush his teeth, studied his smile to assess the need for dental floss, decided that it would be unnecessary, let himself feel annoyed a little too long by the continual thinning of the hair growing on his cranium, laid three ties against his shirt to test the coordination of colours, decided not to wear one at all, but did put the same shirt back on. Before setting off, he gave in to the temptation of a lovely espresso with a generous layer of froth, which he bitterly regretted when he arrived at the chief's office only to discover a few brownish spots staining his sleeve.

"Jesus!" he exclaimed. "How can I be seen in public like this?"

"I know, I know," said the chief. "But don't get all upset. The media are still out of the loop."

"The media?"

"About Poste-au-Chien-Blanc, for God's sake!"

"Oh! Poste-au-Chien-Blanc, yes. I think in my case I got quite the bargain."

The Investor's calm, almost disinterested attitude was somewhat disconcerting to the chief, and it weighed on his mood. He let the moment pass, hoping that the Investor would be tempted to elaborate on his state of mind, but ended up growing impatient with his total lack of urgency.

"That's all you have to say on the subject?" asked the chief.

"I don't know what more I could say," replied the other, in a measured tone. "I have to talk to my advisors to see what I can recoup from my investments."

"Recoup?" fumed Sacred-Bear. "We're losing face, Mr. McClass! And we might lose our freedom as well! It's a one-way trip to Donnacona, this deal we're talking about!"

Breathing heavily, the chief waited for a reaction, a response, some kind of sign to reassure him, but his colleague wasn't listening to him or even looking at him anymore. His vacant eyes calmly roamed from one piece of furniture to the next. After a moment, his eyes settled on his knees, where he found his hands, which he stretched out and continued to stare at, as if they were covered in blood.

"This stain… Good God, it'll never be gone!"

"Precisely, Mr. McClass," agreed the chief, with satisfaction. "We all have the same one now. We're all connected!"

"I'm talking about the coffee on my shirt," said the Investor, in an irritated voice. "As for the rest, all I did was provide you with the capital outlay for the acquisition of infrastructure. What you did with it or what you intended to do with it, I have no idea. I know nothing. If I made a mistake, it was falling for all this."

Chief Sacred-Bear leapt from his chair and resisted the urge to slap the bejesus out of the big prig, which was especially difficult considering the rage that was boiling inside him. Nevertheless, he managed to control himself. "You goddamn, shit-eating liar! You think they're going to let you off so easily? You think the media won't see through your little game?"

"What do you think?" replied the Investor with controlled insolence. "Who is more believable as a poor, gullible victim? The Indian chief who lines his own pockets or the White schoolteacher who used his nest egg to save the little savages?"

"You fucking White shithead!" shouted the chief as he hammered his fist on the desk to mark each one of his words. "You think I have nothing incriminating against you?"

The Investor stood, smoothed the bottom of his shirt and the top of his pants with one hand, passively watching the chief forcefully sweeping all the papers and random objects off his desk, and concluded that the discussion was coming to an end and that, overall, he had prevailed. But he couldn't help swaggering about one last time before leaving the room, as if there were no real satisfaction to be found in having a privilege if you didn't take a moment to flaunt it: "Mr. Sacred-Bear, even if you have evidence against me, which I highly doubt, it would always be your word against mine. And in any world and under any circumstances, the media, just like the judges and the jury and probably even the majority of your brethren, will always side with the little middle-class White guy. It's a fact. You know it. I know it. Everyone knows it."

Jacqueline was hit in the neck by a stapler, narrowly managing to protect the Investor, and escorted him to the door before her boss got into even more trouble. She then hurried to remove, as best she could, the broken cups, crumpled papers, and butchered paintings victims of Sacred-Bear's anger before the arrival of the next guest who, fortunately, was going to keep the chief waiting a tad too long for his liking.

IV

The Banker indeed kept Sacred-Bear waiting a tad to long for his liking, which made the chief somewhat suspicious. The Banker actually worked in the business sector, and contrary to what his nickname might lead you believe, he was not really a banker. As the chief well knew, Vincent Yaskawish trafficked instead in indulgences, while keeping the lion's share in terms of influence. He knew the right people, knew how to beguile them for his own benefit, and steered straight to the heart of the vagaries of politics the way a good navigator does when the wind changes tack, which probably explained his legendary longevity as a member of Kitchike's band council, on which he served under the Tooktoo reign as well as under that of the Sacred-Bear family.

"Where were you?" the chief barked, without standing up.

"Chief Sacred-Bear, you know perfectly well that I have many files to settle before I go on vacation. With the new investments for the sawmill and..."

"The investments? We're on the verge of getting thrown out of our seats, of having our faces plastered on the front page of *Photo-Police* and then rotting in prison!"

"Chief, my friend, I understand what you're saying, but you know that at the end of the day, the economy can't be slowed down by partisan demands. Band business must continue to generate funds for the good of our members and for investors."

The flow of liberal platitudes that the Banker spewed in his face made the chief's head spin. His mannerly affectation of an assimilated burgher suddenly nauseated the chief, who leaned back for a moment to regain his composure.

The gleaming smile that clashed with his swarthy complexion, the snow-white of his tie and his calcified soul, the little greying tuft of hair that matched his suit, and his overall appearance that simulated Wall Street's voracious ranks, everything that helped the Banker easily entice the reserve's voters, docile investors, and seductresses looking for an exotic sugar daddy: All this provoked in Chief Sacred-Bear the most profound disdain. He had tolerated Yaskawish since he entered the arena because he was in need of allies, because the man was already established there, and because he'd proven to be particularly useful. But, today, Sacred-Bear was no longer in the mood.

"Dammit, Vincent! Drop the simpering act for a second, and look truth in the face! Look!" ordered the chief, shoving the photo two inches from the Banker's nose. "Who does it belong to, that pretty little phiz next to mine in the photo? It's yours, so don't play innocent with me!"

Vincent Yaskawish lowered his eyes and stifled a smile. He held his head high but relaxed his shoulders, still acting all holier-than-thou. What he was about to say to the chief in his most candid tone of voice would not please him. "It's only a photo, Chief. A photo in which I appear next to certain unsavoury characters, yes, it's true. But a picture in which I appeared at the insistence of my chief, who sent an email requesting my presence at this meeting, a meeting for which I received nothing *a priori*, no agenda. And I was totally unaware of the subject matter that would be brought up at said meeting."

"Jesus! That project was always *your* idea! You're the one who introduced me to the backers. And you're the one who benefits the most from it!"

"If that were the case, I imagine that my signature would appear on a document," replied Yaskawish coolly. "Or that I would have been invited to subsequent meetings, which could have been proven by any minutes taken."

"Christ, Yaskawish! You're the one who didn't want us to..."

The chief abruptly stopped speaking. His breathing slowed, and the chair shattered under his weight. Briefcase in hand, the Banker straightened his shoulders, plastered his gleaming smile on his face one last time, and left the room, heels clacking and head still held just as high.

V

Lorette Paul, a lifelong friend of the Sacred-Bear family, was known for steering clear of all partisanship. Unlike the various reputations the people of Kitchike enjoyed, Lorette's tended to be based on fact. Mrs. Paul was therefore surprised to receive a summons from the Chief. She hesitated for a moment or two, determined whether she should deign to respond to such an impudent request, then finally decided to let curiosity get the better of her. Although the experience might be disagreeable, she could turn it into an interesting anecdote to romanticize and recount to her girlfriends at the Gas Bar. At her age, this remained one of the only things that still induced her to get up every morning to go to work.

"My lovely Lorette," said the chief, in a tone too honeyed to be sincere, "You know it's not easy to trust someone when you're in my position. So today, I'm turning to you because I know we understand each other."

Jack paused for dramatic effect but more specifically to study old Lorette's reaction, and since she simply looked him straight in the eye and smiled, he assumed that he was in control and continued his monologue. The chief liked very few things on this earth, but he adored the sound of his own voice.

"We understand each other because we see the world the same way. We're honest people. Loyal. To the community, the nation, our family, our friends…"

"Of course, Jack," responded Mrs. Paul as she fidgeted on her chair. "Everyone knows that I've had the same boss since I was 15 years old."

"You and I, we're dutiful," continued the chief. "We have our values in the right place. When we do something, it's never in a selfish way. We are… patriots. True patriots. When we see one of our own living in poverty, we're not afraid to get our hands dirty, to roll in the mud, if necessary, to save our brothers and sisters. But sometimes, there're people who may profit off of our kindness. We act too quickly… We get taken advantage of."

"And you called for me because…"

"I got caught in the trap, Lorette," interrupted Sacred-Bear, his voice intense. "I know that you can understand this. Because it had happened to you, too, when you were younger."

Mrs. Paul stared silently at the chief for a long moment, a question of testing his game plan, seeing how long he could keep playing the role of well-intentioned victim. After 32 seconds of holding his gaze, the little lady was the one who finally flinched and lowered her eyes, which she found most annoying.

"Jack," she said, with a slight air of disrespect, "are you referring to the time I let the young Tooktoo woman watch the cash register while I went to the washroom?"

"I just said that the two of us are the same, that we've experienced the same thing."

Mrs. Paul left the chief hanging, swaying her head from left to right to assist her thought process, when she realized that she'd already had enough of this little game, which was turning out to be as unpleasant as she had expected. There was nothing in it to romanticize, nothing terribly amusing to tell, so she raised her eyes and got straight to the point. "Let's assume that it's true, that we're the same, and that we got swindled the same way. Don't tell me you suddenly feel the need to talk about it. What do expect me to do?"

"You're the queen of the Gas Bar, Lorette. Everybody listens to you, no matter what their political or religious affiliation. You could convince them by telling the truth. That I got taken in by Yaskawish and his pansy racist of a schoolteacher!"

The cat was out of the bag. Strangely, the truth was rather disappointing. Banal and predictable. Certainly nothing to turn into a great novel, hardly even a short story. Lorette thus opted for a more precipitous ending. After all, she had very few days off.

"You're right about one thing," she said in a conciliatory tone. "We all make mistakes. I made one 17 years ago by trusting someone I shouldn't have, and I had to make amends. I repaid Alphonse every penny by working overtime for months."

"But we're not talking about petty cash here," said the chief, his voice suddenly sounding much more acerbic. "Can you imagine the consequences?"

"I'm sure you'll be just fine," she said empathetically. "Whatever happens, I can guarantee you that the legend of Jack Sacred-Bear will live on. Good luck, Chief."

Mrs. Paul rose and walked toward the exit, but none too quickly, just in case a little insult, a few teary eyes, or even a physical assault might come jazz up the end of her story.

Sacred-Bear didn't give her the satisfaction.

VI

Arthur Halloway was the youngest of Difreddi's eight illegitimate sons. As per the boss's own admissions, Arthur was particularly gifted in terms of his business discretion, which explained why he was often the contact or intermediary in his father's schemes when he wasn't too busy getting falling-down drunk in the cellar of his own bar, a dreadful lair full of Goth queers that bore the name of the cuckhold who had given him his last name. Young Halloway would have given Jacqueline a real piece of his mind, but feeling he may have use for it in the future, he simply told her to go to Hell before demanding to speak directly to the chief.

"Hey! Tecumseh, you wanna play with me? You're gonna get burned," he spat into the telephone.

"I don't think you're in a position to threaten anyone, Halloway. You know what I have in my hands?"

"Your limp dick? Fuck off! You think we don't know you're trying to screw us?"

"What are you talking about?" asked the chief, who was clearly shaken. "I wanted to warn you. There's some incriminating evidence that's about to go public..."

"Don't play the innocent if you like your teeth where they are. I know you sent a little Kawish to scope us out. The next time you send a mole in a fancy suit to my bar, pick one who's bright enough not to cruise my little honeypot, okay?"

The conversation took a turn that the chief would never have expected and, since he understood absolutely nothing of what that snot-nosed prick Halloway what spewing in his ear, he decided to put an end to the shameless little conniver.

"Forget about it, okay? I'll settle this with your father."

"My father already knows about it, Sitting Bull. And he says that the deal no longer stands. The project is moving forward, and unless you want to end up singing soprano, you're going to personally make sure it damn well does. But forget your cut. That's finito, you're getting nothing. I'd advise you to keep a low profile and keep your guys corralled like good little savages."

Chief Sacred-Bear would have liked to hurl his anger at this insolent son of a bitch but noted philosophically that he no longer had the strength. Was it fear, this sudden sensation in his gut? This new reversal of fortune would certainly explain it. But no, he thought. No, it was more like a kind of acceptance, a quiet serenity. He was tired, that was all. Since morning, he had been spewing out his venom on a multitude of individuals, and he would gain nothing more by further provoking the Difreddi clan. Jack Sacred-Bear hung up with neither insult nor goodbye.

VII

Big Labelle had travelled the world from east to west and north to south to put the fear of God into pagans and nonbelievers of every background, only to wind up at the end of his career on this minuscule semi-urban reserve, which was undeniably one of the last places in Canada where his holy cross could still inspire fear and respect. Neither his parishioners nor Kitchike's political institutions cared much for the missionary priest. He knew it and basically couldn't have cared less. Loving his neighbour was a strategy of subversion that proved very useful when he wanted to endear himself to the faithful and keep them under the aegis of Rome, but he could easily do without it. Loving his God, on the days when he believed in Him, was enough. The rest of the time, his congregants' fear and respect suited him just fine. In this sense, his vision and his position were not so different from those of the chief, which perhaps explained why the two men maintained a sort of mutual respect characterized by a generalized though extremely polite and complimentary apathy, whenever they met in public.

On that day, however, such was not the case.

"Come in, Father," said the chief, who was watching the reserve's daily activities from his upstairs window. "Have a seat."

Father Labelle studied the chair that was offered him, noted that the armrest considerably reduced the space available, and then concluded that if his backside managed to reach the seat of the chair, he would never be able to extract himself from the seat without damaging his pride. Thus, the priest dragged his elephantine body to the window where Sacred-Bear was standing, each step heavier than the last.

"Mr. Sacred-Bear," said the priest, panting. "You seem to be more preoccupied than usual. What has you so troubled?"

The chief was resting his forehead against the windowpane, his shoulders bowed and his voice faint. He was not the type to let his guard down in front of a priest and especially not in front of Labelle. This man could see the invisible waves of despair and knew how to exploit each drop. Sacred-Bear knew this because it was a skill that he mastered equally well.

Why then had he called for the priest? Of all the men and women on the reserve, why summon the priest if not to use the man's control over the reserve's faithful for his own purposes? This was surely the conclusion of the portly Labelle, whose protuberant cheeks puffed up under a smile that was for the most part quite authentic, and the priest was probably right. A man of this sort could have but one motive, one expectation in adding the priest's name to the list given to Jac-que-li-neh: using the holy terror to lead Kitchike's flock to the side of the saints. The Sacred-Bear side, of course. Except that, for a reason that he found completely incomprehensible, Jack Sacred-Bear felt... something. An emotion. Was it a regret? Some kind of shame? Was it wrong? Was it wrong to use the fear of God to ensure his political survival? And moreover, did he deserve it?

Jack Sacred-Bear was not one to spend a great deal of time wrestling with such ideas. He was not one to have second thoughts. His capacity for self-examination could be summed up in a few circular arguments that featured him at the epicentre around which others were forced to dance. He was an honourable man, so all that he did was honourable, and those who did not share his opinion were either crooked or idiots. He was always right and, if he was ever wrong, he had good reason to be wrong. But at this moment, the big wooden cross that graced Labelle's neck provoked in him a profound questioning that he would have preferred to avoid.

"Father" he said, his voice weary. "I... made a mistake."

The priest's bulging eyes cautiously looked at him, their expression vacillating between empathy and confusion.

"Would you like to make your confession?"

Sacred-Bear hesitated. He didn't know how to play this role, to bend his spine to repent and plead for penitence, as he had often seen his fellow citizens do when they came to seek his good graces. And although his entire being implored him not to trust the priest, he tried to duplicate the posture as best he could.

"I trusted the wrong people, Father. I ventured onto trails with too many twists and turns, but with the best of intentions. I mean, when I became chief, it was to change things. Restore the image of the community and of the Sacred-Bear clan. But I believe I wandered off track somewhere. I went astray…"

"Oh no!" interrupted Big Labelle harshly. "Don't use such trivialities with me," he said as he gesticulated with the entirety of his fat arm. "If you want absolution, you'll have to be more specific: 'My father, forgive me because I lied, I cheated, or I stole,' yada, yada, yada."

Surprised and more than a little irritated by the priest's reaction, Sacred-Bear felt a knot growing in his stomach. He made an effort to ignore both the feeling and the interruption, then answered in a steady voice. "Do you think I'll be forgiven?"

"Are you looking for forgiveness from God or mercy from your constituents?"

"I'd like… I'd just like to get out from under this," confessed the chief, in all sincerity.

"Oh! In that case, you must do penance, my child."

"I don't think a few 'Hail Marys' will save me from this situation."

Big Labelle sized up the chief with his frog-like eyes and then gave him a reptilian smile.

"Probably not," he said as he walked toward the door. "But a vote of confidence for our blessed Church would certainly help me help you."

The chief's bowels clenched a little tighter, and he felt the knot dangerously rise into his chest. Sacred-Bear stood up and went over to the priest.

"What are you trying to say? That you can't help me because I don't show up at church often enough?"

"No, you're a busy man," said Labelle, sounding conciliatory. "You need this downtime to rest..."

"But still..." said the chief, feeling the knot climb into his throat.

"I heard it said that in the Tooktoos' time, the Council refused to let the trembling heretics use the community hall. I was also told that no one was allowed to bring up the subject of pagan rituals at the schoolhouse. You see, these kinds of good deeds would have been especially pleasing to our Lord and to our Church..."

"And if I ever agree to do this sort of... penance, Father, could the Church and its worthy representative back me up and publicly support me during my period of repentance?"

"Oh, come now! Faith is not an election campaign. Good intentions are not enough. It's one's actions that do the talking. You must perform an act of contrition *before* you can be forgiven."

Jack Sacred-Bear did not know how to play the penitent, but he knew the way politics worked and was able to evaluate the opportunities, possibilities, and priorities. He could do the math. And it took him less than three seconds to resolve the priest's implicit request, which he mentally summed up with the formula {a + b + c + d = e}, or:

a) he was in no position to issue an executive order;

b) he didn't have the time to call a meeting of council members to issue a Council directive;

c) the person responsible for the community hall would refuse to obey a direct order. Ditto for the school's Parent Committee;

d) the combined number of traditionalists and Pentecostals was probably equal to or greater than the number of practicing Catholics.

Sacred-Bear raised his chin and came a touch too close to the priest's pudgy cheeks, then got rid of the knot that was tormenting his throat by spitting in his face, "In that case, we'll be meeting in Hell. You're likely to fry there much longer than me, *dear Father*."

VIII

Yvette Sacred-Bear did not enjoy meddling in politics, especially since her younger brother had been in power. But since she benefited greatly from the privileges that his position offered, she had to defer to him and show up as requested. The furtive looks from the people she met along her way, as well as the nervous behaviour of the Council employees, convinced her that all was not well with her brother. Jacqueline seemed almost panicky but remained courteous as always when she opened the door to the chief's office.

"My God, Jack!" exclaimed Yvette when she noticed the pitiful state the room was in. "Have you been vandalized?"

Jack Sacred-Bear, busy picking up a few knick-knacks near the bookshelf, didn't have the courage to look his sister in the eye. He simply gestured with his hand, a signal whose meaning Yvette could not identify, unless it was a meant as sign of surrender.

"Jack?" she persisted, sounding doubtful. "Did you do this?"

"Jesus Christ on a cross, Yvette," he said in a heavy voice. "Just leave it alone."

The woman's wrinkles stretched out, lengthening her face as she awkwardly ran on shaky little legs to slap her younger brother's face.

"Jack Sacred-Bear, you'll watch your language around me. Whatever is happening, you leave religion out of it."

Jack withheld a fit of laughter. He wanted to say that it was too late for that, that he had already sought the help of the Church, that the Church had already refused to cooperate, and that he had finally told the Church's representative to piss off, but the chief chose to remain silent and thus avoid another slap.

The little lady was tickled by Jack's refusal to speak. The Sacred-Bears found little virtue in silence, especially when they were its target. Tight-lipped, Yvette firmly held the chief's jaw between her fingers and pulled his face down so that she could look him straight in the eye when she spoke. Although she'd always been quite petite and was at least two feet shorter than her little brother, she'd never been afraid of him. And she would not accept such defeatism from a member of the Sacred-Bear family.

"Jack, what is really going on?" she asked, without offering any further sympathy.

The chief took his sister's hand in his big, damp mitt and gently pulled it away from his face.

"Whatever I did," he said as he walked toward his broken chair. "It doesn't matter any more. The wind is picking up, and there's going to be some serious turbulence for a while."

Rising to her full height of four feet, two inches, the older woman blocked his way. Realizing that he had no intention of cooperating, she decided to shake him up by whacking him several times with her purse.

"Hey!" exclaimed Yvette. "You may be the chief, but I'm still the eldest in the family. I want to know what is going on. Especially if I'm going to have to clean up your mess."

Jack Sacred-Bear let out a heavy sigh then brusquely said, "Poste-au-Chien-Blanc. Let's just say that the funding..."

"You know the rule," she interrupted. "You do not incriminate the family. I don't want to know what you've done. I only want to know what *can* be done."

The little lady's determination and resilience suddenly restored the chief's energy. His composure was back along with his arrogance.

"Someone spilled the beans. And know someone from Kitchike has gone fishing around the city with certain photos. Showed up at a dive bar for Goth queers. Just recently. This week."

"Was it a Tooktoo?"

"I don't think so. Someone close to the Banker, in any case. Yaskawish is a conniver, but he'd never give up his sources of revenue just to take me down."

"Can we plug the leak?"

"I asked that little good-for-nothing, and it seems not. It's already been made public."

"Do you have support for a different official version? Allies or witnesses that you can buy off?"

The chief just shook his head no. He picked up the photos and held them out to his sister, who examined them nervously before tossing them onto the desk with disgust.

"I wish Papa was still here," said Jack. "*He* would've known what to do. He would've had my back."

"No," said his older sibling, with a haughty attitude. "If Papa were here, he'd still be chief, and you'd be living in his shadow. And even if you'd managed to unseat him, he'd have let you drown in your own shit the better to reclaim his role. He always believed that the position was his by divine right."

"You're not lifting my spirits here, Yvette."

"If you want a pep talk, go ask old Noé. Whatever happens, you're going to stand tall and keep your head on straight like a true Sacred-Bear. Then you're going to summon up all your anger and make each and every traitor pay."

His sister's words penetrated the chief's soul, where they found fertile soil. She was right, obviously. Sentimentalism and defeatism were beneath the Sacred-Bear clan. He had to pull himself together without delay. Nevertheless, he had hoped for a little more concrete support from his sister.

"Can I count on you to rustle up a really good lawyer?"

"Of course, Jack," she said, on tiptoes to kiss his cheek.

She took a few steps toward the door, but before leaving the room, she added "Now that I think about it, I ran into Pierre Wabush at the Gas Bar on Sunday. He was wearing an odd black suit, not his usual sporty attire. I'd start digging there, if I were you."

The chief shouted for Jac-que-li-neh, who ran to his side once again. He scrawled some numbers and some letters on scrap paper, sealed it all in an envelope, and gave it to his secretary.

"I want to see each of these people in my office. Get them here, one at a time. And find me Pierre Wabush ASAP."

Jacqueline nodded her head and left as quickly as she could.

IX

Roméo, the old traditionalist, did not particularly care for Chief Sacred-Bear, nor had he liked his predecessors. He felt very little sympathy for the band's politicians. At best, he saw them as an evil required for management of the community; at worst, he saw them as soulless vultures eroding the nation's cultural foundation for their own benefit. But he was careful to remind himself that deep inside every man, there was a little bit of light, a little divine magic, even in those who preferred to create mayhem. After all, order and chaos were both necessary to the eternal revitalization of the Universe. The two had to dance nonstop to nourish the cosmic circle. Each person had to have his place, even the most unpleasant.

"Mr. Sacred-Bear, can you explain to me why I am here, in your office, instead of enjoying the wonderful spring weather?"

"Stop it, Méo," said Sacred-Bear firmly.

"Okay." The old man reined himself in, losing his smile. "But at least be so kind as to get straight to the point."

"Tell me what you know, and that way the two of us will both save time."

"I know that a rumour has spread like wildfire, from the post office to every home in Kitchike. But since I haven't been there yet this week, I'm not up to date. According to patrons of the Gas Bar, it concerns your imminent downfall. And since you brought me here, and I find you alone, you must be completely out of allies you can trust. That about cover it?"

"Don't you want to know what they're saying? What I've done? If it's true?"

"Not really" admitted Brokenheart. "But I would like to know what I'm doing here."

"It's Yaskawish. He engineered everything so he could fill his own pockets to the band's detriment, and now that we've been caught, he wants me to take the rap."

"Whatever," said the old man, still sounding indifferent.

"You think that's fair? You think it's okay that the Quebec cops are going to show up here and put me in handcuffs while that big faggot gets off scot-free?"

Roméo Brokenheart relaxed. He was not the kind of man who sought out or encouraged conflicts, and even less the kind of man who twisted the knife in a wound. He believed in neither vengeance nor resentment. He got neither joy nor satisfaction from the situation in which the chief found himself. But Old Brokenheart figured that it would have been easier to contain the emotions boiling up inside if only Sacred-Bear had not claimed to have the lofty principles that he had been trampling on with impunity for years.

"Why am I here?" asked Roméo once again, holding back his anger.

"The traditionalists will support me if you speak to them, Méo. They're the only ones who can save me, and you're the only one who can convince them."

The older man's look was compassionate for a moment. Then he sighed.

"Sorry, Jack. What would I be worth as a guide if I used my influence for partisan purposes?"

"Not for partisan purposes, Méo. To save a man from lies and injustice!"

No, he wouldn't dare, thought Roméo Brokenheart, not with me. He wouldn't have the nerve to portray himself as an innocent victim or worse, as a champion of righteousness, truth, and justice. He wouldn't dare open that door, knowing full well where that conversation would lead.

"And why would I do that, Jack? Why would I risk my honour and integrity to try to save you?"

"Because you are who you are, Méo. That's the way you define yourself. Decency, righteousness, good deeds done for their own sake. That's what you preach to the traditionalists, so if you abandon me, here and now, how will you be able to look at yourself in the mirror before you go to sleep?"

That was why Roméo Brokenheart hated politicians. Because despite their arrogance and their total lack of subtlety, despite their shameless and crude way of exploiting people and using them to their own advantage, they still managed to manipulate your thoughts until you doubted your instincts, and then used your own principles and values against you. But Roméo Brokenheart was no longer a child. He was old, too old, for this kind of game. If he preferred to avoid politicians, it wasn't because he felt disarmed by this type of man, but rather because he didn't like the person he might become in their presence. Moreover, Roméo remembered that the only way to remain faithful to himself was to become as clear and reflective as a lake, to echo back to the other his own image. Being genuine and true. That was a sure bet, one proven by experience and the passage of time.

"I'm nothing to you but a simple tool. You think you know me, and you think you can manipulate me with rhetoric?"

"Méo, it's not manipulation, it's in your genes. It's a fact. Look at your cousin Jac-que-li-neh. I'm a bit rough on her, but she doesn't take it personally. She does what she thinks is right. She's a Brokenheart, just like you."

"So I have to cover your ass because that's my place?" said Roméo resentfully. "That's the role my family has to play, serving the ruling class? Serving the Sacred-Bear clan? Your father would be so proud to hear you talk like that."

The chief closed his eyes, as much to take the hit as to control the rage rising in him. *My father? How dare he compare me to my father?* James Sacred-Bear had ruled with an iron fist for more than 20 years. He had been an unrelenting brute, a warlord, the real deal. Jack was not his father, but he was a Sacred-Bear and that was quite enough for him. He inhaled deeply and opened his eyes to stare at Old Brokenheart.

"And Diane? You know very well that Diane would want the truth to come out, and for Yaskawish to pay for this conspiracy!"

Old Roméo's heart stopped beating. A flood of emotions spilled into his being and sent him reeling. That's where the conversation was headed, inevitably. He'd known it from the minute he'd set foot in the chief's office. No matter what he might have said, no matter what he might have done, the conversation would have gone in this direction, of that he was certain. Nausea made him stumble backwards, but he quickly pulled himself together. Roméo tried to control the tone of his response, but he had to fortify his emotion-battered voice so as not to whisper.

"Diane… Diane is gone, Jack. My sister left us exactly five years ago, the night when your son-in-law, who was flat-out drunk, ran her over with his car. Naturally, since you fired all of the cops, including the chief of police, to keep the whole thing quiet, no one ever knew the truth and never would. And you have the nerve… to talk to me about Diane? To talk to me about truth and justice?"

"You owe me one," insisted the chief, halfway between arrogance and desperation. "If I hadn't lifted the ban on sweat lodges that the Tooktoo's young Baptist brought to a vote, you'd have been ruined in court. So you owe me one, and it's the time to pay up."

Old man Brokenheart had never doubted the chief's somewhat psychopathic nature, but his total lack of empathy at that moment revealed a character even more vicious than he'd imagined. Once the element of surprise had dissipated, once the force of the sting had worn off, a touch of pity poked through the dawn. But it was only a mirage, he knew, an emotion meticulously planned in the chief's manipulative calculations. That was the sign he needed to conclude the conversation.

"Yes, I know, Jack," said Roméo firmly but gently. "So I'm going to do one thing for you. Just one. I'm going to go into the woods, and I'm going to pray for you. I'm going to ask Diane and the Ancestors to help you do a little thinking. And I promise you that if things work out that way, I'll come visit you in prison. I'm not a Tooktoo. I'm not a Sacred-Bear. I don't abandon my own."

Old Roméo left the chief's office, his heart shattered, but his mind at peace. He knew that, somewhere between the far West and the radiant heavens, Diane was smiling.

X

Uncl' Noé, that tall string bean with the weak bladder, seemed to have shrunk considerably in his sweat lodge. That's what Sacred-Bear thought when he saw the old man dragging his feet into the office. Safe to say that time had not dealt kindly with him, its ravages having creased the skin around his bones, from head to toe. Tall though he was, today he walked with knees up and back bent.

"You have some pretty nice restrooms here, dear nephew," said old Uncl' Noé, smiling widely. "When your dad was chief, we didn't have that kind of luxury. Just an old outhouse between two spruce trees."

The chief stood to welcome his uncle, and after a hearty handshake and a heartfelt embrace, he invited him to sit at the desk.

"You've got quite the armchair here, Jackie my boy. I bet there are a few ministers who've farted on this chair. If my old mutt Cajou were here, he'd have hours of fun sniffing at the upholstery."

The chief chuckled. He always enjoyed being with his old uncle, even at his advanced age. Perhaps it reminded him of simpler days, his early childhood, and the myriad grimaces and monkeyfaces the old string bean had made for him in order to brighten days that were otherwise bleak and lonely.

"Uncle, I'm glad you agreed to come see me. I'm going through a difficult time, and I need your wisdom and your advice."

"Oh! Jackie-Boy, you should've warned me. I'm afraid I don't have much left of either one of those," he said as he lit a clumsily rolled cigarette. "But I may have a few crazy stories saved up, if that might make you smile."

"Like the time you cheated in the portage race?" asked the chief, who laughed heartily. "I can picture you strutting around in front of those sexy kitschy girls, the burlap bag light as air, listening to that big Tooktoo boasting of your prowess before he found out you'd orchestrated the whole thing just to make him lose face in front of all the nations and the sponsors at the pow-wow. Yes, that's a great story, Uncle."

While the chief had certainly put some oomph into it, old Noé clearly did not share his enthusiasm. The wrinkles on his face, now obscured by a cloud of smoke, refused to form anything resembling a smile.

"You think that's the moral of the story, Jack? You think that I did all that to heap shame on Tooktoo? To make him lose his sponsorship?"

"That's what Papa always said. And besides, that's the story the Tooktoos always peddled. It's not for nothing that they hate us so much, those sons of bitches!"

After a few seconds of silence, the chief insisted on having an answer, although Jacqueline, who was secretly listening at the door, could certainly have testified that since he had never actually asked a question, it was somewhat incongruous to expect a response.

"Why did you do it then? It wasn't just for the girls?"

"Of course not, Jack. But you must admit that it's pretty nice getting checked out by the sexy young things. Sexy... Sexy what...?"

"Sexy kitsch, Uncl' Noé, sexy kitsch!"

Old Noé burst into a fit of giggles and in doing so, clearly swallowed a huge puff of smoke because he began to choke in earnest, even as he continued to chuckle.

"Yes, yes, that's it, sexy kitsch! That is really and truly the right expression. You won't find a better way of saying it than that, dear nephew. The little fringed panties and little laced-up breasts, those were the good old days, weren't they? When did our young ladies turn all that in for sweatshirts and sweatpants? Exactly when did that happen?"

"That's not the question, Uncle!" said the chief, clearly irritated. "I asked you why? Why the bag of sand? Why bring down the pow-wow and the sexy-kitsch costumes and the big Tooktoo fair if it wasn't to shame them?"

"Because it was funny, Jack. They were so ridiculous. They'd created an imaginary universe that was un-be-*liev*-a-bly sad. I just wanted to prove it to them with a big dose of humour, Noé-style."

"Papa was right, in the end. It was still to attack the Tooktoo regime!"

"Which one of us is the old and senile one? It wasn't against the Tooktoos! It was just a bit of comedy to restore the balance of cosmic forces in Kitchike. Things were getting too fossilized. Sort of the way they are today, Jack," said the old man as he stubbed out his cigarette on the desk.

"Today?"

"Yes, yes! This very day!"

A shiver slid between the chief's shoulders and ran down his spine. Jack Sacred-Bear hesitated a second before pursuing his line of questioning. He was afraid of the answer the old prankster would give.

"And what did you do today, Uncle?"

Old Noé broke into another round of guffaws, so doubled over with laughter that he was incapable of answering. A deep-seated rage overwhelmed the chief, who lost all semblance of civility.

"Noé, you incontinent old beanpole! What've you done this time?"

"I, oh, I, I faked a big trip!" said Old Noé between two bursts of laughter.

"I hope you realize that it may have been your last," threatened the chief.

"No, no, not *my* trip," said the older man. "*Your* last trip. And thanks for the note of farewell delivered to the reserve's mailboxes!" he chuckled, tossing a postcard at the chief's face.

Gripped by a hilarity bordering on the unnatural, Old Noé ran out, holding his stomach with both hands and leaving a trail of urine behind. Jack Sacred-Bear did not feel like laughing. He picked up the card that the old fool had flung his way, then saw with horror that it was indeed a postcard. On the shiny side was one of the photos that he had discovered in the Council's mail that morning. His business dinner at the ranch. There he was with the Banker, the Investor, the Lawyer, and the other. The other one whose name must not be spoken. And on the other side, a brief note ending with a fairly successful forgery of his signature:

Dear Kitchike,

A little souvenir of my trip to Poste-au-Chien-Blanc. My associates and I are hoping for plenty of profits at your expense. Always a pleasure to use your collective interests to our advantage. Be docile and virtuous!

Your chief,
Jack Sacred-Bear
First Nation of Kitchike™
(all rights reserved)

XI

"The man with three to five first names" bent his back to slip into the office, raising his long arm in an exaggerated form of greeting, but feigning a mischievous smile failed to hide his anxiety. It was not every day that the chief invited you to his office. In truth, Jean-Paul Paul Jean-Pierre did not remember ever being summoned by the chief or by anyone else, other than Dr. Dentures' secretary and perhaps his ex-wife's lawyer. Oh, he was so naïve! Everything was becoming clear now. All that had been nothing but a distraction tactic while the dentist secretly met with his wife. Was Dr. Dentures perhaps trying to revive the ploy to steal the favours of his new lady friend away from him? Jean-Paul Paul Jean-Pierre smiled. He couldn't be fooled again because he no longer had a lady friend. But that didn't keep him from showing the chief that he had fully understood the ruse.

"I'm not with Julie-Frédérique anymore," said Jean Paul Paul Jean-Pierre, frowning. "So it's pointless to go on with this game. Your friend from the neighbouring town already pulled that on me."

"You know about Mr. McClass?" asked the chief in surprise.

Mr. McClass? That was to be expected, thought Jean-Paul Paul Jean-Pierre. His White neighbours, or rather, the inhabitants of the neighbouring town, were certainly all in cahoots when it came to seducing the girlfriends of autochthonous Aboriginal Indigenous Amerindians who were members of the Kitchike First Nation. Nevertheless, he had always believed that his former schoolteacher was not the kind of man who would participate in such uncivilized schemes.

"So?' repeated the chief.

"That surprises me," replied Jean-Paul Paul Jean-Pierre. "I always believed that my former schoolteacher was not the kind of man who would participate in such uncivilized schemes." This time he said it out loud.

"I understand where you're coming from. Personally, it's beyond me. How can someone abuse the confidence of the good people of Kitchike that way?"

"It happened to you too?" asked an astonished Jean-Paul Paul Jean-Pierre.

Jean-Paul Paul Jean-Pierre didn't know if the chief had a girlfriend. The chief's wife had left him many years ago, more years than Jean-Paul could count on two hands because he had lost his right pinkie in a work accident, back in the days when he was working. Since then, he had never seen Sacred-Bear in the company of a woman, but since the chief spent a great part of his life travelling beyond the reserve, he might have met and kept a woman somewhere else and kept it a secret from everyone. Everything was becoming clear now.

"Where did it happen?" asked Jean-Paul Paul Jean-Pierre out of curiosity.

"At the ranch, of course. I didn't see it coming," said the chief, sounding quite depressed.

Jean-Paul Paul Jean-Pierre didn't know how to respond to the chief or how to reassure him. He took a moment to collect his thoughts, a long moment of reflection that, as usual, ended up dwindling away like the tail of a fish, first a goldfish and then a seahorse. Even if he wasn't quite sure if it was actually like a fish at all, the latter specimen had a more interesting tail than a plain old goldfish. He had already seen a seahorse at the zoo, and it seemed so happy paddling around in the water.

"And were there seahorses at the ranch?" asked Jean-Paul Paul Jean-Pierre. "I really like exotic fish."

The chief knit his brows. He definitely wondered where Jean-Paul Paul Jean-Pierre was going with this. But that was of little importance because that was not why he had summoned him.

"No," replied the chief, "But if you like exotic fish, I know just the place where you can see some."

Jean-Paul Paul Jean-Pierre's eyes suddenly lit up.

"Really?" he said with a grin. "In the neighbouring town?"

"No," said the chief. "In Florida. With everything that's happening now, I need to take my mind off things."

"I get it, Chief. With the invasion of black holes and the other plagues of Egypt that are spreading out through Kitchike, no one can blame you for wanting to take a little vacation."

"Tell me, Jean-Paul, do you still have your old Mazda? I need a chauffeur."

Jean-Paul Paul Jean-Pierre couldn't believe his ears, so he relied on his eyes, which confirmed what he'd heard: Jack Sacred-Bear, Chief of Kitchike, had invited him to vacation with him in Florida! Never would he have believed that he would one day be so honoured. He pictured himself sharing a table with the chief in a big Southern restaurant, savouring seahorse or some other expensive edible creature, and perhaps even appearing next to the chief on a postcard sent to his fellow autochthonous Aboriginal Indigenous Amerindian members of the Kitchike First Nation. Lady Luck was finally smiling upon him, and he was not the type of guy who let such an opportunity slip away.

"I'm your man!" exclaimed Jean-Paul Paul Jean-Pierre emphatically as he sprang to his feet.

Jack Sacred-Bear gave a satisfied smile and said, "Go park behind the building and help me carry my bags down. We're leaving!"

XII

Pierre Wabush did not answer his emails, not even his goddamn Facebook messages. Jacqueline asked some of the chief's men to make the rounds of the village but held back the urge to tack *Wanted: Dead or Alive* posters on the community's poles.

According to Jakob, Wabush had headed into the woods and wouldn't be back for a few days. But a few days would be much too late for the chief's liking. After hesitating for quite some time, Jacqueline decided to simply cross the name off the list, hoping that she wouldn't have to pay the price for this unexpected but fortuitous disappearance.

XIII

Jacqueline Brokenheart was as surprised to find that her own name appeared on the list of those summoned as she was to notice that the chief hadn't cut it up into separate syllables as he did when he spoke to her out loud.

When she entered her boss's office at the time indicated on the slip of paper, she realized that he had vanished. On his desk, she found four cardboard boxes full of papers along with a note in his handwriting:

Make it all disappear.
Absolutely everything.
Even this piece of paper.

Jacqueline wondered if "everything" included the packets of $20 bills left on the pile of boxes, but to avoid getting blamed later for having misunderstood the instructions, she discreetly stashed them in her brassiere before beginning to shred the rest of the paper.

And all of it, absolutely all of it, disappeared.

EPILOGUE(S)

Five minutes to midnight in the Kitchike woods. The moon had risen late, but there it was in the middle of the sky, and I still couldn't find a little shadowy area to hide in. From whom, from what? Maybe just from myself, after all is said and done. Pierre Wabush, you big dope, why didn't you just go home to sleep?

What's done is done, and what do they actually have against you?

Not much.

I should be happy, but to tell the truth, I'm really not. I never thought that Old Noé would flip out like that. No one can say that the old buffoon lacks imagination. If I'd known he was such a talented pickpocket, I'd have paid more attention.

Fuck it all. It's over, right?

One way or another, it's all settled. No more Sacred-Bear, no more Prince of Canada, no more noxious arrogance, no more political power going to the highest bidder. Peace, righteousness, and justice will begin to grow again in Kitchike's fertile soil!

Hah! You'd have to be pretty naïve to fall for that. Such is not the case with me. Nah, I know very well what lies ahead. The media will all talk about the Kitchike Council's duplicity, public opinion will assume that we're all crooks, and then who is everyone around here going to blame? Sacred-Bear? Yaskawish? The Mafia? The law firms that finance the little princes' scams? No, the guilty party will be the one who breaks the code of silence. The blabbermouth, the pariah who dared bring everything out in the open. Pierre Wabush. The one and only. Not the big beanpole who sent the postcards.

Some people would hasten to pin the blame on Old Noé to save their own skin, but I'm not one of those "some people." I'm not the kind of person who blames old folks for our transgressions. Especially not the most justified.

Others might believe that I should be thanked, but I'm not foolish enough to hope for preferential treatment. No, now, everyone will be suspicious. Not just the Sacred-Bear family. Everyone. There won't be anyone left who'll dare speak to me, not for quite some time. I'm going to be radioactive, socially contaminated.

One thing for sure, after this episode, I'll never get another job with the Council. Because even without Sacred-Bear, Kitchike is still Kitchike. There's no room for pariahs here. Either you bow your head and shut your trap, or you quit the community. There's no Plan C, unless you're an old fool. But me? I have no intention of leaving. I'm going to stay here to remind all those swindling viceroys from the reserve's backwoods that they're being watched. I'm going to be the Batman for the poor, the self-proclaimed ombudsman for the underprivileged, the goddamn Trickster of myth. If I must, I'll even tattoo "Fuck you, big chief" on my forehead and strut down the streets of Kitchike until I'm senile and incontinent. Old Noé won't live forever. Someone will have to take over for him.

Just as I notice that hunger is beginning to gnaw at my gut, the miracle that I had expected, if I'd actually believed in something, pulls me away from my masochistic delusions. Above the top of the trees, on the other side of the river, lights are flying up toward the firmament. Two comets dance around each other before ascending the steps to the sky where they are swallowed up by a toothless celestial mouth.

Wow.

I may be closer to senility than I thought. Maybe it's a sign. But since there's no legend associated with it, I'm just going to lean up against a tree and hope to dream about a little tenderness. Maybe I'll even park my pickup in the little Yaskawish's garage. She might not have any steering, but at least with her I don't have to explain a thing.

⊙⊙⊙

Five minutes to noon in the Old Town, live from Alphonse's place.

A Thursday in April similar to the others, only sadder.

Even the blazing sun can't drag a smile out of Kitchike. It just makes our shadows even longer, drowning our embarrassment in obscurity. It's not that we're unaccustomed to bad news. No, I think that we could have our own televised newscast. As Stephanie says, the problem isn't so much the misfortunes. Rather it's the lack of alternatives, our inability to think ahead, encourage hope, and imagine things differently.

Elizabeth says it's because of colonization and our fabulous "democrappy."

I'm not sure what that means. I didn't stay in school long enough.

What I do know is that Jack Sacred-Bear's duplicity reached heights rarely seen around here. It created a whole feeling of dejection, some kind of collective shame whose burden we all must share. If only we could share power in the same way.

The Sacred-Bear clan lost its champion. Once it lost its leader, the disciples couldn't come to an agreement about his successor. No chief, no interim; the ministry had to call a new election. The Tooktoo clan gloated all week long. They'd already begun to celebrate their victories by the time the campaign got underway. For the moment, Max is happy – the never-ending parties improve the sales of cases of beer. That's not what I find the most delightful. Because at Alphonse's, an election means that all the candidates will come strut their stuff and preach their usual stupidities to a clientele too scared to let anyone know which side of the ballot was going to receive their "X." If only I'd been able to finish school, I'd have been able to spare myself this whole adventure, then disappear into the city for a while. But no, I'm stuck here.

In Kitchike, if you don't have an education, you can scrape by with a job at the snack bar, at one of the craft boutiques, or at Alphonse's Gas Bar. If you're a girl, that is. As for the guys, they have other possibilities, but I can't say that I envy them. The shops on the reserve make you old before your time, in both body and soul. Just look at Jean-Paul Paul Jean-Pierre, and you'll see what I mean.

Hey! Jean-Paul disappeared with his pickup, at the same time as Sacred-Bear and Pierre Wabush. Mrs. Paul started a pool. She's taking bets on which of the two is responsible for bringing Jack down. Let's be honest, most of the girls bet on Wabush. Personally, I just hope that nothing happened to him. I like Pierre a lot. Under different circumstances, we might have spent some time together, shared more than a few nights. The last time I saw him was at the première of Teandishru'. He seemed happy, pleased to have come to encourage his young friend. Teandishru' didn't stay long. He disappeared after his last show; off he went with a young woman, a new flame, in search of a fairy tale. I wonder if he heard the news. It's going to be hard to digest, even for the local superstar. He's going to be asked a lot of questions while he's on tour.

Yeah, me too, I'd like to be able to get out of here. Go to university, as far from Kitchike as possible, to cram my head full of concepts each more abstract than the next. When my little Waso is big enough, for sure I'm going to do it. Spending my hours and my days reading and writing: That would be a welcome change.

Maybe I should start by writing a journal. Have to get all of these stories out of my head. I sometimes find my universe so sad. Maybe if I put all this down in writing, I could turn it into a great novel...

Who knows? Perhaps that would ease my troubled heart.

EXILE EDITIONS
RECENT RELEASES

AMUN
A GATHERING OF INDIGENOUS STORIES

SELECTED BY MICHEL JEAN

TRANSLATED BY KATHERYN GABINET-KROO

In the Innu language, amun means "gathering." Under the direction of Innu writer and journalist Michel Jean, this collection brings together Indigenous authors from different backgrounds, First Nations, and generations. Their works of fiction sometimes reflect history and traditions, other times the reality of First Nations in Canada. Offering the various perspectives of well-known creators, this book presents the theatre of a gathering and the speaking out of people who are too rarely heard.

Authors: Natasha Kanapé Fontaine, Melissa Mollen Dupuis, Louis-Karl Picard-Sioui, Virginia Pésémapéo Bordeleau, Naomi Fontaine, Alyssa Jérôme, Michel Jean, Jean Sioui, Maya Cousineau-Mollen, and Joséphine Bacon.

"Ten different stories set in multiple epochs and contexts, offering glimpses of lives that provide a wider view and understanding of Indigenous experiences."

—*Montreal Review of Books*

BAWAAJIGAN
STORIES OF POWER

CO-EDITED BY NATHAN NIIGAN NOODIN ADLER
AND CHRISTINE MISKONOODINKWE SMITH

Ranging from gritty to gothic, hallucinatory to prophetic, the reader encounters ghosts haunting residential school hallways and ghosts looking on from the afterlife, bead-dreamers, talking eagles, Haudenosaunee wizards, giant snakes, sacred white buffalo calves, spider's silk, a burnt and blood-stained diary, wormholes, poppy-induced deliriums, Ouija boards, and imaginary friends among the many exhilarating forces that drive the Indigenous dream-worlds of today.

"This is, overall, a stunning collection of writing from Indigenous sources, stories with the power to transform character and reader alike...the high points are numerous and often dizzying in their force..." —*Quill & Quire*

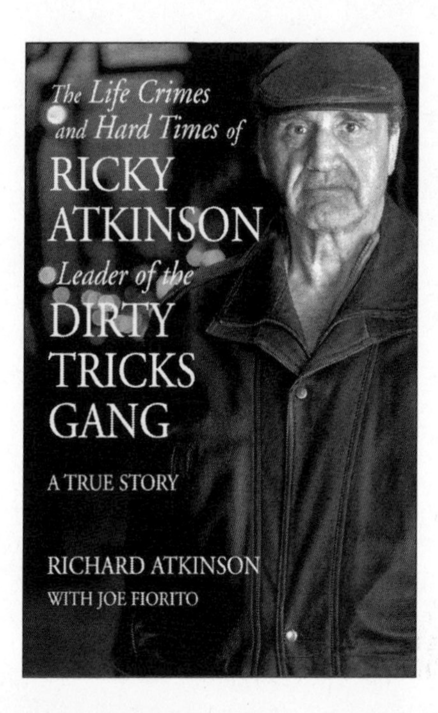

THE LIFE CRIMES AND HARD TIMES OF RICKY ATKINSON: LEADER OF THE DIRTY TRICKS GANG

RICHARD ATKINSON WITH JOE FIORITO

This is the life story of Ricky Atkinson, who grew up fast and hard in one of Toronto's toughest neighbourhoods during the social ferment of the 1960s, '70s, and '80s. His life was made all the more difficult coming from a black, white, and First Nations mixed family. Under his leadership, the gang eventually robbed more banks and pulled off so many jobs that it is unrivalled in Canadian history. Follow him from the mean streets to backroom plotting, to jail and back again, as he learns the hard lessons of leadership, courage and betrayal.

"Atkinson's memoir is as riveting as true crime gets... It is also a reckoning of the city's racist sins. [and he] makes the convincing connection between societal prejudice and crime in minority communities. It's a revelatory and fascinating story told from a rare perspective." —*Publishers Weekly*, starred review

THE SILENCE

KAREN LEE WHITE

In *The Silence,* with the Yukon as a canvas, White engages in a deep empathy for characters, emergent Indigenous identity, and discovery that employs dreams, spirits, songs, and journals as foundations for dialogue between cultures, immersing the reader in a transitional world of embattled ethos and mythos. Her first novel is a *cri de coeur* that lives alongside Smart's *By Grand Central Station I Sat Down and Wept* and Kogawa's *Obasan*.

Karen Lee White holds the torch brightly as a new and powerful voice, her style and sensibility encompassing the traditional and the contemporary.

Includes (on the inside cover) a CD of the author/songwriter/musician's original music.

COYOTE CITY / BIG BUCK CITY

TWO PLAYS

DANIEL DAVID MOSES

First Nations playwright and Governor General's Award finalist Daniel David Moses is known for using storytelling and theatrical conventions to explore the consequences of the collision between Indigenous and non-Indigenous cultures. *Coyote City* and *Big Buck City* are the first two in his series of four City Plays that track the journey of one Native family between a world of Native spiritual traditions and the materialist urban landscape in which we all attempt to survive.

"*Coyote City*... so powerfully conveys how Canada and the future look to young Native men and women who choose the company of their own dead in preference to life in a society with no role or place for them." —*Globe and Mail*

"*Big Buck City* is a strangely powerful, disturbing piece of work...life and death and money and magic swirl around each other...an amusing but familiar farce [turns] into something more powerful and more difficult to pin down." —*Globe and Mail*

YO! WIKSAS? / HI! HOW ARE YOU?

ART: RANDE COOK TEXT: LINDA ROGERS

"Squirrel Nation and discerning kids everywhere will be delighted with this fun, fast-paced, and rollicking collection of poems by Linda Rogers, accompanied by silk screen images by Chief Rande Cook. *Yo! Wiksas?* is an innovative fusion of Kwakwaka'wakw art, Kwak'wala terms, and delightful English-language verse."
—Richard Mackie, Editor, *The Ormsby Review*

Illustrated conversations are the Indigenous way of showing rather than telling, and these conversations between Isla and Ethan – son and daughter of Chief Rande Ola K'alapa (Cook), a much loved artist of mixed European and Indigenous decent – and their invisible friend Siri touch on bullying, environmental protection, and inclusivity – all very important topics for children. Isabel Rogers, also a kid, is part of the storytelling process.